Dragon's Fury

Dragon's Fury: (The Chronicles of the Fifth Kingdom

Fantasy Series

series)

by
Brian D. Meeks

CHAPTER ONE

A sudden hush from the patrons in the Third Eye Tavern drew Trilina's attention. It could only mean one thing—a newcomer.

Getting up from her mahogany desk where she'd been finishing the books for the month, she wandered over to the door. The entrance to her office afforded her a good view down into the main area. Both her sisters were working down there: Frilina behind the bar and Brilina taking drinks and food to tables.

Swaggering up to the bar was a young man she'd never seen before. He made a beeline for the bar stool nearest Frilina.

"What'll you have, stranger?" Frilina asked.

"My name's Denton, and I'd like not to be a stranger."

"Well, darling, er, Denton, my name is Frilina, and

that's my sister Brilina, and we're delighted to meet you... friend."

Brilina wandered up behind him, leaned in close and said, "Who is our new friend, Sis?"

He took a look at her, then he looked back at Frilina, and for a moment didn't move. They had that effect on people. "Hi, I'm Denton," he said again.

"Have you tried our brandy?" Brilina asked, winking at her sister.

"I would love to try the brandy. I've never met such lovely twins."

"We're not twins," they replied together, stating the fact without malice or annoyance.

Denton looked at them both for a long time, his expression a mix of confused and quizzical. "Are you fooling with me?"

Brilina leaned in, bringing her mouth to his ear. Despite not being able to hear, Trilina knew what she was saying. It always happened. They offered the stranger a bet about them being twins—their version of fun.

"You look identical to me," he replied. "What sort of bet?"

Frilina put her elbows on the bar, resting her face in her hands and said, "It's simple, you'll tell us you believe we're not twins. If we can convince you to admit you were wrong, we win, if not, well, you'll make a fair bit."

He reached for his coin purse and said, "You're going to convince me. All I have to do is remain unconvinced, and I win?"

A hush settled over the bar. Everyone knew what was coming next.

"Yes," Frilina said, voicing that thought.

"How are you going to convince me?"

"It's simple, we put this blindfold on you, and kiss you three times. I think you'll find that our kisses are so vastly different that you'll know we couldn't possibly be twins."

"How much?"

"How much do you have?"

Denton pulled out his coin purse and dropped it on the bar.

Brilina said, "That sounds like one hundred twelve coins, and from the tone, I'd say they were gold."

"Well, you've got a good ear, and yes, it's exactly one twelve," Denton said with a smile.

Frilina said, "We don't want to take your last ducat, so let's say a hundred?"

"Done."

With the ringing of a bell, the bar went still.

"We have a wager," Frilina announced and pulled a silk scarf out. She handed it to her sister who put it across his eyes and spun him around on the stool.

The whole bar yelled "One!" This was Trilina's cue to join them. Fighting back a grin at the familiar game she padded silently down the stairs.

She watched as Brilina took his face in her hand and gave him a long wet kiss. When she stepped away, he swayed.

Frilina had walked around the bar by then.

The locals all yelled, "Two!"

She wrapped her arms around him and, with gentleness, she pressed her lips against his.

Denton said in a low voice, "Wow, but I'm not convinced."

No longer hiding her grin, Trilina placed a hand on his shoulder. As she moved around him, she ran her fingers through her hair.

"Three!" everyone called.

Her turn. Trilina let her cheek brush against his before she followed her sisters and kissed him. This time he almost fell off his stool.

"Yes, that was different, but your considerable prowess in the ways of kissing doesn't make me believe..." he trailed off as he took off the blindfold.

Before him, Brilina, Frilina, and Trilina stood, side by side.

"I'm Trilina," she said. "Although most people call me the Third Twin."

Denton didn't say a word.

He opened the pouch, counted out twelve coins, and set them on the bar. The rest of the bag he handed to Trilina and said one thing, "I've never lost a bet and felt like I had won, before. Now, I'll take that brandy."

The bar erupted.

He was now a local.

Trilina gave him a peck on the cheek and returned to her office.

CHAPTER TWO

The silence surrounded Marl as he picked up another fallen chair and righted it. Grabbing the empty tankards from the table beside it, he headed back to his bar. Just barely, at the edge of his vision, Marl caught sight of a figure by the door, cloaked and standing in the shadows. He tried not to show his fright. The stranger had made no noise entering.

"We're closed," he called over his shoulder.

"Are you sure?"

The figure stepped forward, but Marl didn't need to see under the hood to know who it was. He recognized the voice. An avalanche of thoughts filled his mind while his body eased behind the bar and continued tidying up.

"Why are you here? You never saw fit to visit before now." He picked up a cloth and wiped it across the top of the wooden bar, soaking up the spills and mug-sized circles left on the worn, unvarnished surface.

"It's back, Marl."

Finally, he looked up at her, sitting on the nearest chair as he did.

"Are you sure?"

The hood nodded, and it came another step toward him, the cloak flowing to the side for a second to reveal the armor and sword underneath.

Exhaustion hit Marl, making his legs shake. His body had held up for the last three years, carrying him through the routine as he did the job of two alone, but this was too much.

How could it be back?

Realizing he still clutched the cloth, he put it down on the nearby table and sighed. Would he not be allowed to run his tavern in peace?

"You'd best get us both a drink and tell me how you know."

She didn't move until she pushed her hood back and looked at him. "I've not come alone," his sister-in-law explained.

He nodded, resigned. Nothing else she said could make things worse.

As she turned to open the door and call out, there was a jolt, a deep pain in his chest, the sight of her so familiar.

Opening his mouth, he intended to tell her to get out. That he didn't care or want her there, but the moment passed, and the words never came.

A person, more boy than man, followed her back

inside, each of them equally garbed in cloaks, the clank of his metal armor told a tale.

Marl didn't know her friend. His limbs were calm, but his face told all Marl needed to know. There was fear in his eyes.

It truly was back.

The darkest point in Marl's life had started at a time when he still had a wife and kid, when his arms were strong and legs unyielding, when he hadn't known what lay ahead. It had been for glory and riches that he had left with his sister-in-law and the others. Marl hadn't known he had all the wealth in the world just beneath the golden ringlets of hair on the little girl that had said, "I'll miss you, Daddy."

No bar towel could wipe away that memory. No amount of drink, either.

The father inside him taking over, he got to his feet again. They'd need food and drink.

By the time he'd put together a tray of bread, cheese, and ale, they were sitting by the fire. His sister-in-law had placed several fresh logs on and stoked it back to life—something he hadn't expected Elora to know how to do. Three years ago, she'd had servants to do that for her.

"Right. Start from the beginning," Marl said, as he put everything down in front of them. "And don't leave anything out."

"Jenson here saw it first," she said, pointing to the kid, a skinny boy dressed in a loose-fitting set of chainmail that was scuffed and rusted in places. He tried to lift his chin, to look brave and confident, but all it served to do was draw attention to the thin goatee that didn't suit someone so young.

Marl gave him a nod, anyway, trying to encourage him to begin his tale.

"I was up Antwick way," he said, his voice quivering only a little, "watching my uncle's sheep. Something I do when one of his shepherds is sick. I made a campfire like normal, got myself all cozy, the sheep settled by the east wall."

"Let me guess. You had a bit of old Rupert's home-brew to help keep you warm?" Marl said, interrupting.

The kid colored but nodded. "Only the one, mind you. I would have had more, but to be honest with you, I'd been up late a few nights, and I slept more than I drank."

Marl nodded, wondering when he was going to get to the point. No part of him doubted this kid had seen it. The fear in his eyes and the way his hands shook as he clutched his mug of ale said enough, but he knew others would want to ignore him. They'd pretend he saw things while drunk. People liked to act like nothing wrong was going to happen.

For the land he loved, a good deal of bad was going to happen.

Marl had done his bit, and it had cost him, but he would face it all over again, if only to get a good night's sleep one last time.

CHAPTER THREE

Trilina had half an hour.

It was her twenty-eighth birthday. It also happened to be Brilina's and Frilina's. Of course, they were both younger than her, but Brilina only by five minutes and Frilina by eleven.

Like they did every year, there would be a party this evening, but she still had a few more minutes before she finished the tavern's books and headed downstairs to join her sisters.

They'd been working all day, giving the regulars free drinks and chatting more than usual.

Trilina could hear it in the background now, but she had one more task for the day. Going to the locked cabinet in the far corner of her office, Trilina pulled out the last of eleven identical tomes. Inside the collection of large books was an entry for every single day from her fourteenth birthday. Today was no different.

Written in her mother's familiar script were instructions, thoughts, encouragement, and lessons ranging from how to grow basic crops to what she and her sisters should look for in a husband.

She was sitting where she always did at this time of day. Trilina read today's entry.

I know I've been gone now as many years as I was blessed to raise you, but I know you and your sisters will have flourished. Enjoy your birthday and celebrate this last year of training your magic. You've earned it.

Your sisters are growing wiser each passing day and week as well. I always hoped to be there to teach you all, but you've done wonders in my place. I'm proud of you.

This next year will test all of you, but do not let fear keep you from taking on its challenges. Your sisters will be fine without you, and you must allow yourself to follow the call of adventure.

Before this next year is out, your journey will begin. A sign will tell you when the time is right to start to balance the scales.

Happy birthday, my dear Trilina.

Trilina sighed as she sat back in the chair. Her birthday message each year always spoke of the future, the year ahead and going on some adventure, but what that adventure entailed and what particular scales needed to be rebalanced the books never said.

This was always the time of year she missed her parents most. Her mother's visions had allowed her to leave a great gift within these books, but it didn't replace the relationships the triplets had lost.

After Trilina put the book back in her secret stash, she pulled out the very first volume. Tucked into the first page of the first book was a letter. It had arrived on her sixteenth birthday. Each sister had received one.

Hers had told her where to find these tomes and what fate had befallen her parents. It was only a year ago that Trilina had found out she shared her mother's gift for magic. This eleventh tome was full of instructions on how to train. And it wasn't finished.

The clock striking the fifth hour of the afternoon signaled the end of Trilina's alone time. If she didn't go down to the bar, her sisters would come up to find her.

Tucking the books back, Trilina locked the cabinet and stepped away. The business could also wait another day. It was time to begin her twenty-eighth year. And time to start looking out for a sign.

CHAPTER FOUR

A chill ran through Marl as he stepped out of his tavern. He was only a couple of steps behind Elora and Jenson as they moved to the small stable to get the horses ready. Each of them carried a bundle of provisions to pack into their saddlebags.

No one knew for sure when they'd be back.

Before heading to the stable, Marl used a nail to fasten a small piece of parchment to the door. His inn would be closed until further notice. He could only hope nothing happened to the building while he was gone.

He wanted to stay and protect the building and all the memories it held, but he knew if they didn't leave and face their enemy now, he might lose the inn anyway.

"Are you sure you want to chase Aldrei?" Elora asked, her face turning to him as he stared at his little sign.

"Yes. If I don't, not one of us will sleep safely at night. You remember what it was like last time."

When a dragon settled in the area, it was only livestock that were threatened at first: cattle, mostly sheep in their case. But after dragons came worshippers and cultists. And dragons grew. Some even decided to lord their presence over nearby humans.

His little inn might not be in danger right away, but as soon as Aldrei had established himself, and his worshippers had followed, they'd slowly devour or enslave more and more of the country. Marl couldn't allow it. Not again.

Elora was the first to pack and ready her horse, a light brown mare that whickered as she mounted.

"I'll head back to the homesteads and warn the farmers, then gather my equipment. If I don't find you later today, I'll meet you on the road between Antwick and Trentfri."

"You don't want us to come with you?" Jenson asked, his voice shrill for the first word, unmasking his fear. It took all Marl's self-control not to roll his eyes behind the kid's back as Elora shook her head.

Without another word she rode off, a trail of dust kicked up on the dirt track with every pounding beat of the horse's hooves.

"Right, we'd best be off ourselves. We don't want to waste the light." Marl tested the strap before swinging up into the saddle.

"No, I guess not," Jenson replied, but he didn't

move from beside him.

"You don't have to come too."

"No. I do. You're going to need my help."

"You're not wrong there. We barely beat Aldrei off last time. And he was only a wyrmling then. I hate to think how big he is now," Marl replied, not thinking until he saw Jenson's eyes widen further. He had made it worse.

Somewhere inside, Jenson found enough courage to mount the gelding in front of him. Giving him an encouraging nod, Marl dug his heels into his horse and steered it in the opposite direction from Elora's fading dust cloud.

"Let's go find Kal. We'll need his bow if we're to present a threat to Aldrei." The words were unnecessary. They'd already discussed this part of the plan, but Marl didn't want to stop talking, now he'd found someone to talk with, as he enjoyed it. Too many of his nights and mornings were lived in silence, alone. Jenson might have barely been old enough to be an adult, but he'd already shown himself to have some guts about him, and Marl knew Jenson's father wouldn't have trusted him with the flock without good reason.

"So, how's Nikarus? He still hopes to win the fair at Antwick with his Bratarian sheep?"

Jenson let out a chuckle. "I didn't think you'd recognized me."

"You've grown, but I know one of Nikarus' kids when I see one. How is everyone?"

"The family is well, but worried."

Marl nodded, glad they'd already been informed. The sooner everyone knew Aldrei was back the better. He gritted his teeth, feeling an old anger rise inside of him. Some dragons didn't know when to die.

"I was expecting to see your little Arla scampering about the inn. She's twelve now, right?"

The question caught Marl off-guard, making him frown. Trying not to think about it, he shook his head. "Would have been twelve in the spring," he eventually replied.

Jenson's mouth dropped open as the meaning dawned on him. "That must have hit Kenna hard."

"She followed Arla to the grave. Bandits..." Marl couldn't continue. His throat tightened. Another word would have betrayed the depths of his grief. If only he'd been there to protect his wife and child and not to fight Aldrei the first time.

"I'm sorry." Jenson looked away, the mood somehow more somber and oppressive than it had been when he'd only had a dragon to face.

Marl tried to think of something else to say, but his thoughts didn't want to leave the memories. Painful ones of coming home to an empty house, knowing that what had happened could have been prevented, had he just been back in time.

"Come on," Marl said, giving his horse a nudge to make him go faster. "We won't have found Ilran by nightfall if we don't pick up the pace."

Jenson followed in silence, leaving Marl to emotions he'd pushed away for years.

When Marl had returned home from defeating

Aldrei and protecting their lands, he'd found his small family dead and his angry sister-in-law waiting for him to explain why he hadn't been there to protect them. All the celebrations he'd planned had fallen into nothing, Elora not making sense beyond the only words that mattered: "they're dead." From then on little had mattered.

After doing all he could to hunt down the killers and turning up empty, Ilran had found him drowning his sorrows in some back alley tavern. He didn't remember much of that night or of the weeks between losing hope of finding the bandits and waking up in Ilran's hut, but he'd not touched a drop since.

It was ironic to have become an innkeeper, but it had kept him busy. Each day he got up, served travelers food and drink, gave them a roof over their heads, and cleaned up after they were all gone. And each day he was too busy to think about his life before.

As they rode on, Marl stole a glance back to the inn as it faded into the distance. It was the refuge he'd built in more ways than one. Aldrei would regret coming back; Marl would make sure of it. If it weren't for the dragon, he'd still have a family. He'd have always been happy.

Marl clenched his fists and fixed his eyes on the road ahead. This time Aldrei wouldn't survive.

***

Both Marl's legs ached, and his stomach had been rumbling for an hour before the sun was at its peak.

I've gone soft. Not enough training or hunting, he thought, surprised at how unfit he'd become. The inn had kept him busy, but nothing compared to the time on the road, food rationed to what could be preserved for weeks or killed along the way. It was an entirely different way of life.

Marl hadn't thought he'd missed it. At least, not while he worked, but now he was back in the saddle, contemplating going back into battle with old companions, he found he had. It all seemed familiar, almost right.

Beside him, Jenson fidgeted on his horse, shifting his weight and adjusting the reins every few minutes. It was clear he didn't have much experience on horseback.

Fighting back a sigh, Marl considered pausing early for lunch. They'd not packed much, but it would give them a moment to stretch their legs and allow the horses to rest. But that would make the afternoon ride longer. This time he couldn't prevent the sigh that wanted to escape.

"Nearly lunchtime," Jenson said. "Should we start looking for a good spot to stop?"

A grin crossed Marl's face as he nodded. He wasn't the only one thinking of getting some relief, but the cold rations in his pack didn't provide much of a comforting thought. Still, they weren't stale, and there had been many a day he'd had to eat hard bread and scrape the mold off the cheese before he could eat it.

The memories of old journeys, many of them in good company, made his smile broaden. Yes, he'd missed this far more than he'd realized.

Jenson tugging on his reins and slowing his horse brought Marl back to reality.

"There's a good place," the kid said.

He pointed towards a small grassy area to one side of the path. It wasn't anything particularly special, but there was a ring of stones and a darkened patch of dirt that made it clear someone else had used it as a place to rest.

They walked the horses over and tied them to a low tree branch. Marl tried to ignore the ache in his legs and back as he pulled out the rations stashed in the nearest saddle bag and sat down beside Jenson.

It wasn't long before they were both filling their stomachs, the horses grazing as well. It may have been only a light meal, bread with the last of the strawberry jam, but it tasted terrific after riding most of the morning.

"What is it, kid?" he asked, noticing Jenson was staring at something.

"Thought I saw movement," Jenson replied, his voice hushed, and his knuckles whitened with his tightened grip.

Marl raised his eyebrows, surprised the shepherd was spooked so quickly, but when his horse snorted and swished his head back and forth, Marl knew something wasn't right.

Standing up, Marl scanned the horizon, but other than the breeze blowing gently through the trees, they seemed alone.

Damn it, Marl. Too Alone. No bird song.

He drew his sword, glancing at Jenson just long enough to see him pick up on the possible threat and do the same. Whatever was out there, it didn't show itself right away, making Marl wonder if he imagined things.

Stupid fool, he thought. *You're too jumpy and too rusty. Only two years ago you'd have known if there was a threat or not by now.* Lowering the tip of his sword, Marl shook his head. Whatever had scared the birds off, it wasn't coming at them or hiding nearby.

Marl had just turned back to Jenson to encourage him back on his horse when he heard the piercing sound of a crossbow bolt and the thud as it hit the tree to one side of him. It took his brain a moment to catch up as he watched the shaft quiver, embedded in the bark. They weren't alone.

"You're surrounded and outnumbered," a deep growling voice said from over Marl's left shoulder. "I'd advise you to…"

The two men locked eyes, both recognizing one another in an instant. Aldrei's most prized fighter stood just off the road, coming closer, his large sword raised. He snarled, distorting the tanned ruddy face. It was just like Marl remembered.

"You," he said. "Thought you'd be dead by now."

"I could say the same," Marl replied, pulling his small shield off his back and slipping it onto his arm. The dragon worshipper had aged, but he could see the grip on the sword was no less fierce, and it held steady, pointed out at Jenson.

"New recruit to your heathen ways?"

Marl considered not answering, as four more fighters, these younger, a strange light in their eyes, fanned out behind their leader. This wasn't fair to the kid. He'd only brought Marl a warning, but Jenson moved into his field of view.

"There's nothing heathen about our ways," Jenson said. "We just don't believe dragons are gods."

"That's what they all say. Let us teach you both a lesson."

The armor-clad fighter advanced as the four men behind drew various weaponry from beneath their travel cloaks. Marl clamped his mouth shut over the curse words he wanted to utter and charged to the left of the chief cultist.

I hope you know how to fight, Jenson, he thought, as only two of the lackeys and their leader focused on him despite his aggressive move.

As they passed each other Marl parried an attack, flicking his opponents' blade back and turning underneath. The motion ended with the tip of his sword inside the next man.

There was a gurgle as Marl pulled it out, but he could do little more than glance at the unfortunate cultist. He'd picked the wrong dragon to worship.

The clang of more steel coming together sounded to Marl's right as his shield took the next crossbow bolt. At this close a range it was powerful enough to drive the bolt head right through, the tip barely missing his arm behind.

Dodging another thrust from the leader forced him away from Jenson and put the cultists between them.

Marl frowned as he saw the other crossbow-wielding fanatic shoot towards the young shepherd. It took the lad by surprise, embedding itself in his shoulder. He grunted but kept his feet.

Unable to help, Marl countered another attack and feinted to the right as if he was rushing to Jenson's aid. As their leader moved that way to block him, Marl pushed to his left, feeling a muscle in his leg tense at the strain of battle.

Despite the pain, he kept up his momentum, knocked aside the crossbow pointed at him and ran the man through. He didn't have time to pull his sword out of the dying cultist before he was charged from the side and knocked off his feet.

His armor and shield both took the brunt of the blow and dug into his skin, cutting him in several places. He rolled to the side as a sword flashed past his head, and he pushed himself up onto his feet.

"You're getting slower as the years pass," the leader taunted as he swiped towards him again.

Marl said nothing.

Behind him, swords clashed, once, twice, and then a pain filled howl as Jenson fell another cultist.

The leader and remaining cultist struck. Marl parried the heavy blow from the leader and dodged the other thrust. From his right, he saw Jenson lunge at the cultist and run him through.

It was now two on one. Marl and Jenson stood

ready, though Jenson was a bit wobbly. Marl's lungs burned, his legs ached, and it had been a relatively short fight. His mind raced, trying to remember the name that went with the face. It came to him, Cauldor.

"Your friend looks like he's seen better days."

"He's fine, Cauldor. And he'll look better than you when we're finished."

Cauldor sneered. "You remember my name. I'm not sure I ever knew yours or cared. And when your body is rotting here in the forest, it won't..." and he struck.

The speed threw Marl back. Jenson swung, but there was little strength in the attack and Cauldor merely put up a gloved hand and caught the blade, tearing the sword from Jenson's hands. Jenson collapsed.

Marl stuck a blow that was heavier than Cauldor expected, and the leader staggered back.

With a roar, Cauldor brought an overhead attack, spun after blocking, and swung from the hip.

The counter from Marl and a massive kick to Cauldor's midsection threw him back.

Jenson let out a terrible groan.

"Your man is in bad shape," Cauldor said. It must have been the poison on the bolt.

Marl looked down.

Cauldor struck again.

The exchange lasted many blows, but neither could land. For a moment, it seemed Marl might have worn down the cultist leader, but another sorrowful moan from Jenson was just the distraction Cauldor needed, and he said, as he bolted into the forest, "Your future will be in the chain."

Kneeling beside Jenson, Marl asked, "Can you get on your horse?"

"I think so."

"I know someone who can help, but we've got to ride hard to get there. I'm going to pull out the bolt."

To his credit, the boy didn't even flinch when Marl pulled the bolt from his shoulder. The crimson started to flow.

"We need to get you out of that armor. Here, have some water."

Marl helped Jenson free himself of the chain mail. From his saddlebag, he pulled bandages and a flask of whiskey. He took a pull from the flask and said, "Okay, take a bit of this, while I bandage up that shoulder."

Once the bleeding stopped, Jenson managed to mount his horse. Sweat poured from his forehead, and he gave a weak nod.

Off they went, pushing their horses to their limits. For an hour they rode until they reached a stream, where something startled Jenson's horse. The violent bucking threw him into the water. The shock of the cold brought a moment of life back to the fading Jenson.

"We don't have time to chase your horse," Marl said, holding out a hand and pulling Jenson up behind him.

The sun approached the end of the world, and the forest light was dimming, when Marl saw the cottage.

CHAPTER FIVE

The kettle bubbled over the fire. Raina Heliot stirred the pot and watched the rider approach. "Callista, come here."

Raina's silver hair flowed about her shoulders, looking radiant despite her many years. Her short stature and small frame made those who didn't know her underestimate her power. Those who did know came only with respect and reverence. Her eyes were clear and bright, their vision perfect, but she played the part of an old woman like a master thespian.

The horse stopped, and she squinted at their guests. "Who is that there?"

"It's me, Raina, Marl Adhemar."

The cottage sat at the edge of the high trees which bordered the capital of Trentfri. Brilliantly crafted of stone and wood, the home had a quaint elegance, which made it stand out. A cobblestone wall ran around the house and garden. When night fell, the torches would light the wall and cast the whole property in an angelic glow. The silver witch had an eye for beauty in all things.

"Well, you're a long way from the inn," she said waving a spoon at him.

"I need your help. Jenson here has been poisoned. He's in bad shape," Marl said.

From the cottage came a young woman, who said, "Let me help."

"This is my granddaughter, Callista," Raina said, still stirring the pot.

Jenson, barely conscious, slid off the horse. Sweat poured from his face. His body quivered with convulsion.

Marl hopped down and put a shoulder under his arm. They carried Jenson into the cottage and lay him on a cot in the corner.

The fire in the hearth and the smell of lilac put Jenson at ease. A small table held a row of herbs, which Callista had been chopping. There was a pitcher of water, from which she poured a glass for Jenson and helped him take a drink.

Still carrying her spoon, the old witch smacked her granddaughter and then Marl. "Let me through. I need to get a look at the boy. And bring me the ephobala, riccumeric, and uddeomille."

Her granddaughter pulled up a door to the cellar and descended the steps.

"Now, young man, can you speak?"

"Yes," Jenson whispered as his body shook.

Raina touched his head. "Is your vision blurry?"

He shook his head no.

The witch pulled a pin from her hair and said, "Can you feel it when I poke you here?" and pricked his shoulder.

"Yes, the shoulder," Jenson said, his eyes now closed.

"That's a good sign that there isn't any deadness. We need to clean this wound, though. Marl, take the kettle off the fire and grab another. Fill it with water and let me know when it boils. The well is around to the side," she said with a wave of her hand.

Marl did as he was told.

Callista returned from the cellar, "Gran, we don't have any uddeomille."

"Stay with him," Raina said and went outside.

The twilight gave way to night. The forest hummed with chatter from the tiny creatures that lived in the branches. Far off, over the walls of the city, a faint bell rang—pops from the fire mixed with the rich cedar smoke. Raina added a couple more logs to the blaze.

Marl turned and asked, "Will he be all right?"

"It depends," she said, picking up the pot that now sat next to the fire.

"Is that a potion you were brewing when we rode up?"

"It is a stew. No magic, just dinner," she said, dipping the spoon in and holding it out for Marl.

He tasted. "I've not had anything that good since…"

"I know. I was sorry to hear about your family. She was a good woman," Raina said. She got a plate and filled it with stew. "Take a moment; eat a bit. You may have a long night ahead of you. We're out of uddeomille. It's rare. I'll make a list of a few herbalists in town, but I'm not sure any of them will have it in stock. You may have to ride to Antwick."

Marl ate the stew. "We were heading to Antwick tomorrow, after looking up a friend here in town. When I find this herb…what's it called?"

"Uddeomille."

"When I find it, will it be enough to get Jenson back on his feet?"

"Eventually, but he won't be in any shape to wield a sword, if that's what you're asking. It might take a few weeks before he's even out of bed…or maybe until he's in the ground. The sore around the wound looks pretty typical, but there should be numbness. I'm not sure of the type of poison used, so his fate I cannot predict, except to say without the uddeomille, he will certainly die."

Callista closed the door to the cottage behind her. Her dress was simple and white, but with an elaborate blue and green embroidery. She wore silk slippers and moved like her feet barely touched the ground. She had her grandmother's eyes, was a few inches taller, and kept her smooth white hair tied up in a bob over her head. A few strands hung in front of one eye. "He's sleeping, now."

Raina said a few words and the lamps along the wall lit up with warm orange flames. She looked at her granddaughter, who saw it, too. "Something's wrong, Marl, I can see it in your aura. It's more than the injured boy."

"Aldrei is back."

"And why is any of that your concern? Let the army deal with it. There are plenty of soldiers who do little more than march and drink. Their swords and spears need the work."

"General Darnek would throw bodies at the beast until they're all dead and doubt he would even wear out Aldrei. On the battlefield, against men of war, he'll win the day, but he doesn't understand dragons."

"Well the five mages, then."

"By the time they could all agree on a battle plan, we'll be worrying about Aldrei's offspring."

"It seems you're trying to settle a score," Raina said, getting Callista a plate of stew.

"Maybe...probably, but the fact remains he's six years older and who knows what sort of havoc he might bring down all around us."

Raina sprinkled something on her stew and took a bite. "You know, I season the rabbit, which is what makes it taste so good."

"I should probably get going. Thanks for the stew."

"Go saddle up the bay, Callista. That poor horse of yours has had enough for one day. And you're down a man before you even get started. Have you thought about that?"

"I'll find a sword for hire."

Raina shook her head. "You need to pay

attention."

Marl looked confused.

"Signs are all around. And they're telling a story. I don't like where it's heading."

Marl put his hand on her shoulder. "I appreciate the concern. Thanks for the horse, and I'll try to hurry. If I have to ride to Antwick, I'll send word. Now, where are those herbalists?"

She disappeared into the cottage and returned with a scrap of paper, just as Callista brought the horse around. "She's a little spirited, but she'll do what you ask."

He took the paper, thanked Raina and Callista, mounted the horse, and headed toward the city gate.

CHAPTER SIX

The guards gave the slightest of looks as he rode through the city gate. They were probably too young to remember the last time the city had needed to defend itself.

Off in the distance, he could see the five mage towers. Beyond that, the keep, with its imposing black walls, peered down on the city with a reassuring dominance.

A hauler pulled a cart filled with garbage down the street. They were the hardest working and least appreciated citizens. Nobody talked to them, but the streets were clean because each night they came out under cover of darkness and toiled until sunrise.

Marl acknowledged the poor sod pulling his load by way of a nod. He flipped him a copper coin. "Can you tell me where to find the Dancing Daisy?"

"Aye, governor, it's on the other side of the city, in

the Dark Alley. Are you sure you want to be shopping at this hour?"

Marl flipped him another coin and handed him the paper. "What about these two places?"

"Sorry, governor, but I ain't so good at the reading," and handed back the paper and coin.

"No, keep the copper. I need the Seed and Leaf and MaCall's apothecary."

"Those are closer. MaCall's is one street up, and then you head into the Mansion district. It will be locked up tighter than a bank at this hour. The Seed and Leaf is on the Mage Tower Plaza; you can't miss it. You might find someone around. I couldn't say."

"Thanks," Marl said and eased the bay along.

He hadn't been to the capital in many years. The streets looked the same as he remembered. What he didn't expect, or remember, was the gut punch he received when he turned left onto the Main Street that ran up to the five towers. There it was, the Imperial Cross Roads Inn. The most elegant of its type in the kingdom.

Marl had saved for over a year before he asked her to be his wife because he wanted to take her here on their honeymoon. The night they arrived, he had been nervous about more than their wedding night. It was clear he didn't belong as he stood in line at the desk as an Arch Duke and his family checked in.

Before that moment, he'd believed he wasn't afraid of anything in the world, but when Marl saw her eyes scanning the lobby with such pure joy and fascination, he imagined the staff looking down their noses at them. And it would break his new bride's heart.

When it was their turn, he stepped to the desk, and a middle-aged man with a thin mustache greeted him warmly. There were no sideways glances.

Marl thought back. *What was his name?* It bothered him he couldn't remember. Every detail of Karlina's dress, though, that was still there in his memory. She had made it herself with the help of her sister. Everyone from their small village raved about how beautiful it was, but that wasn't the moment she would talk about for years to come.

Waiting patiently in line behind them was a duchess. When they turned to follow the bellman to their room, the noble lady had grabbed Karlina by the elbow and said, "That's the most beautiful gown I've ever seen."

It was that moment. The look on her face would be the one Marl carried with him into battle. It was why he fought the dragon. It was in their daughter's eyes the day she was born.

The rest of the three days was a blur. The Imperial Cross Roads Inn staff treated them like the highest born in the land.

Roderick! It was Roderick at the desk.

The bay moved Marl through the streets. His mind was lost in the past and didn't notice a dirty face darting in and out of the shadows behind him. The Seed and Leaf was dark. Marl dismounted and knocked on the door, but nothing stirred inside. He pounded harder, in case they were asleep. It was an emergency.

Not a sound.

When he turned to get back on his horse, he saw eyes peering out from behind a stack of crates. Marl wasn't in the mood.

He mounted the horse and urged it forward with urgency. The bay responded, and they cantered through the streets toward MaCall's Apothecary. It took little time to arrive at their gilded door. The hauler was right, it was locked tight, and nobody came when he used the massive knocker.

The mansion district was unique among the major cities. Built on a tabletop flat section of land, made mostly of stone, the original designer had used stone carvers to remove the massive blocks needed for the mansions in a specific way to leave behind hundred foot deep, thirty feet wide canyons—each mansion built atop its piece of the stable stone platform.

All along the street, beautiful bridges adorned with family crests arched over the chasms to the homes. Stone walls surrounded each property to give it a feel of being its little castle.

People marveled at the mansion district. The king applauded the designer. And then the designer surprised them all when he rerouted the river coming down from the mountain. The chasms filled and became his signature, now just called the canals. It was indeed a work of art.

Marl looked back. He couldn't see the eyes, but he was sure someone followed him.

When he got to Dark Alleys, he asked another hauler where to find the Dancing Daisy.

Like the others, the door was locked, and nobody answered.

The eyes appeared a little way off, set in a dirty face, and a wiry body. "What you need, mister?"

"I don't give beggars any coppers."

"I ain't asked for any coppers."

"Why are you following me?"

"You looking for something. I know how to find things. Maybe you need help?"

"How can you help me?"

"You need something from Gwendolyn's shop?"

Marl looked at the kid, must have been in his late teens. "What's your name? I don't need a thief."

"I ain't no thief. Er, well, I am a thief, but I do not steal from my friends," he said sounding hurt.

"You know the owner?"

"Better…I know where to find her. You want Gwendolyn to open her shop?"

"It's an emergency. I need…" and before Marl could say another word, the lad had run off down the street.

Marl tried knocking one more time.

When he turned around, the wiry boy and a cherub of a woman were walking toward him.

"Oi, it's been a busy night. More customers than when I was open. What can I do for you?"

"I need some…uh…damn it," Marl swore. He should have asked Raina to write down the name of the herb, too. When had his memory gotten so bad?

Gwendolyn pulled a key from her pocket and opened the door. "Come on luv; we'll figure it out."

Marl opened his coin purse and pulled out a couple of coppers, but the lad was gone. "Who was that boy?"

"Ah, that be Henry. He's a good lad. A little daft, but he's always helpful. Now, what was it you needed?"

"It started with a 'u' and is rare. Something for a healing mixture. Raina said it was unlikely you'd have some."

Gwendolyn got a twinkle in her eye as she showed him into the shop. "Was it uddeomille?"

"That's it! Do you have any?"

"That old witch is always bugging me to get some. It ain't easy, but you're in luck. I got in a few ounces just yesterday. A bit pricy, though."

"What do you need?"

"Three gold."

"How about two gold and five silver?"

"Since it's for Raina, you've got a deal, but you tell her I did you right."

Marl handed her the coin and then dropped in a few coppers. "Could you see that Henry gets this?"

"He's a good boy. I'll make sure he gets it."

CHAPTER SEVEN

Matilda grinned as she struck a chord on her lute. She'd tuned it to perfection. The instrument in her hands was worn, the varnished wood now rough in patches, but it played as sweetly for her as it once had for her father.

As she strummed, she tried not to think about what she'd recently come across. All those ruined trees broke her heart, and there was that feeling in her stomach, like a knife twisting around only, she imagined, less painful. It was a feeling she got every time something was going to happen. Her mother had called it a sort of second sight and told her to listen to it.

Her father had told her it was something he felt, something he channeled into the music. In the end, she'd listened to her father most. So here she was with his lute and both her parents gone. No one had been left in the camp when she'd got back. She'd only wanted a moment alone after weeks traveling with them. Now she wanted them back.

Alone, she didn't dare follow where she suspected they'd gone, however. They were not dead—Matilda's gut told her that too—but they were gone into the Fog. And she didn't know why.

Matilda was still strumming on the lute, her mind drifting as she sat in front of her small fire when she heard the sound of hoof beats on the dirt road. At first, she thought it was a mirage, but when a cloaked rider came into sight, riding a young mare, Matilda stopped her playing and got to her feet.

Waving and calling, she stepped away from her fire, but the horse continued to hurry along.

Almost at the last second, the rider yanked the reins and brought the mare to a skidding halt.

"Damn, girl, I almost ran you down."

"Sorry," Matilda said, not expecting to be met with such anger, or to find the rider was female, her hood tumbling down as she got off her horse. It revealed an armored woman, chestnut hair down below her shoulders, and bright blue eyes filled with intense emotion.

"What are you doing out here alone?" the woman asked, her voice brusque and business-like.

"Everyone disappeared. Went into the Fog, I think."

"Oh..." She said, taking a look at Matilda and the pony she'd tied to the nearby tree. "Well, I need to rest a moment. Why don't you tell me what you know, and then we can carry on together."

Matilda raised her eyebrows, surprised at the kindness that had replaced the earlier impatience.

"I don't know. My family was traveling with the merchants. We wanted to head north for the winter. Visit the city. We're players, you see." Matilda held up her father's lute as she realized she was waffling.

"You were attacked?"

"No. My parents just vanished."

"Vanished?"

"Yes. I went to gather some berries," Matilda lied, not wanting to admit she'd been sulking. "When I came back, they were gone. And the trees were funny."

"Like something had shredded them, funny?"

"Yes. Exactly like something had shredded the trunks." Matilda looked at the woman as she replied. This woman knew something, but instead of asking any questions or telling her anything, she fell silent, staring into Matilda's fire.

"Right. We'd best get back on the road. You should come with me." The woman grabbed some dirt and chucked it onto the fire, making it sputter and go out.

"I don't know you." Matilda frowned, the deep twisty feeling still in her stomach. "Or where you're going."

"I'm Elora, and I'm going to the capital. I won't make you come with me, but there's a dragon in the Fog, and either he or his cultists took your family. If you want to see them again, you'll want to get on your horse and ride with me."

"It's a pony," she pointed out, not sure she liked being told what she ought to do but doing it anyway. "And I'm Matilda."

"Well, Matilda, I'm glad I found you."

Elora was on her horse again before Matilda could respond. She wasn't sure the feeling was mutual yet. This woman was strange, even if she appeared to be trying to help.

Taking her time, Matilda remounted her horse. Making sure her father's lute was slung safely over her shoulders, she nodded to Elora that she was ready to travel again.

It was all the encouragement the woman needed to dig her heels into the mare's flanks until she was flying down the road again.

Matilda's poor pony struggled to keep up. It didn't seem to slow Elora down, however. She rode hard and glanced back at Matilda twice in several hours to check she was still behind. As darkness began to descend and the sun disappeared behind the trees her pony's stamina waned, and she watched the gap between them widen. Matilda called out when Elora was so far ahead that she couldn't see her, but it was too late. She couldn't hear.

The twist in her gut worsened, but on she pushed the pony until she saw Elora ahead. She'd stopped by a small path off the road that wound into the forest.

"I need to see a friend," she said when Matilda came close enough to hear. It was the only explanation she received before Elora handed her the reins to the horse and jumped off.

Matilda watched her jog down the path, passing several stacks of stones that marked the route every few meters until the trees and evening darkness obscured her view.

Despite not being able to see where she went, Matilda continued to look in the same direction. With any luck, this mysterious woman wouldn't be long.

A light appeared, coming from what must have been the open doorway of a wood cabin. It illuminated the building through the trees for a couple of seconds before the door closed.

With nothing else to do, Matilda counted out the seconds as best she could. Somewhere around six hundred, she lost count, distracted by a bird flying out of a nearby bush. She sighed, her fingers going numb where they gripped both reins. The cold of the night was setting in, and this wasn't how she'd imagined spending the evening.

I hope you're all right, wherever you are Mom and Dad, she thought. *And I hope I can find you again.*

Sure that she'd waited as long again, Matilda found herself considering tying Elora's horse to the nearest tree and continuing on down the road. Either that, or going up to the cabin herself, but in the dark, she wasn't sure she could trust herself to find it.

With the closing in of night, she could only see the first pile of stones, and no matter how much she didn't want to be waiting, she couldn't bring herself to get down from her pony and walk towards it. Her indecision ended with a flash of light as the cabin door opened once more. Again, it disappeared, but now Matilda felt hope that the woman was returning. She let out a breath, seeing it puff a white cloud in front of her as Elora reappeared, in her gloved hands a loaf of bread, steam rising off of it.

Elora tore the loaf in half, handed Matilda a share, and took back the reins to her horse. "There, that should help keep off the cold night. We need to ride further tonight if we're to catch up with my brother-in-law any time soon."

Matilda merely nodded as she bit into the hot, soft bread. It had been a long time since her last meal, and the bread more than made up for the angst she had felt while alone in the darkening forest.

"That was the last person I needed to see about this dragon. They all need a warning," Elora added, offering more of an explanation than Matilda expected. "Not that they all believed me." Not waiting for Matilda to finish eating, Elora pushed her horse onward again, also ripping bites off her portion as she did.

After having rested, her pony was somewhat refreshed, and Elora set a less relentless pace anyway. In the dark, it would be far too dangerous to push their mounts too fast. They would be more likely to stumble or sprain a leg if they caught a stone or tree root.

"Where are we going?" Matilda asked, when Elora slowed enough to let her pony pull alongside.

"Trentfri," she replied, not looking at Matilda. "They'll need our help to convince the General that the threat is real."

"But it's still a long way ahead."

"Yes, because I spent most of the day riding in the wrong direction. But fate led me to you, and that means something."

"It does?"

"Yes, you survived an encounter with a dragon. And you have every reason to want to see it defeated. Fate has chosen you to help us at this moment."

Matilda frowned, not sure how she felt about the idea she was fated to help in some great war. She just wanted her parents back, but as her pony trotted on through the night, Matilda suspected her objections wouldn't matter.

***

The sun was starting to show on the horizon when Matilda first noticed Elora slow her horse. They'd paused to let their mounts rest just twice through the night. Each time for only a few minutes.

The second time Elora had urged her back into the saddle, Matilda had protested that she was tired. Several times she'd grown so tired her eyes had closed until she'd slipped enough to jolt awake.

Now that the forest had begun to grow lighter once more, and bird song filled the air, she felt awake in a weird sort of way. A little fuzzy, as if her judgment was off, her eyes not entirely keeping up with the movement of her head. Also elated, almost like being high or drunk, but not exactly that.

It was the first time in her life she'd gone a whole

night without sleep. Matilda couldn't decide if she liked how it felt or not.

As Elora slowed her horse to a trot, Matilda noticed she looked from one side of the road to the other, searching for something. They traveled like this for several minutes, Matilda wanting to ask what it was she looked for but not daring to break the silence.

Matilda spotted the clearing at the same time as Elora. Someone had kept a small area of the forest clear of trees. A semi-circle of cutoff tree stumps sat beneath a willow branch canopy. In front of them lay two simple, but elegant chairs, each carved out of a single piece of wood. It was almost romantic in a rustic sort of way.

Not needing to be told that was where they were heading, Matilda tugged her reins and guided her pony through the few trees between it and the road.

Elora was the first to dismount, still looking about her. Leading their mounts, they walked to the edge of the canopy, but whatever it was her companion sought, it wasn't here. Nothing was.

"He should have been here by now," Elora said, not explaining who he was.

As long as it wasn't this supposed dragon, Matilda didn't mind. She sat on one of the stumps, not feeling like she should sit on one of the chairs. They looked like they were reserved for people more important than her. The kind of people who arranged meetings here, not those who ended up at them because they had nowhere else to go and needed help finding their parents.

"I guess we wait for him, then," she replied when Elora simply stared at her. It was almost as if the older woman hadn't even thought of this.

"I guess so. It wouldn't be the first time."

"Waiting for him? Or sitting waiting here?" Matilda asked, finally letting some of her curiosity out.

"Both... Actually."

Matilda blinked her surprise but didn't speak. She wanted to see if Elora elaborated, but the woman went to her horse and rummaged in the saddlebags.

She pulled out a small wooden charm, dangling from a leather cord. It looked as rustic as their surroundings.

"I was given this the last time I was here, carved from the same wood as everything around you. It was his idea. Something so simple, but so elegant in its way."

"You loved him?" Matilda asked, but this only made Elora chuckle.

"Not me. My sister. But it was coming here that made it clear how much he loved her. I could see why she chose to settle for him... He'll be here. This spot is where they got married."

No wonder it's romantic, Matilda thought.

"Rest," Elora said a moment later, tucking the necklace back inside her shirt. "We need to rest while we can."

For a moment Matilda frowned. Despite riding all night, she didn't think she'd be able to sleep. She took the offered blanket anyway and wrapped it around herself.

While they waited, there was little else to do.

***

A hand over Matilda's mouth startled her awake. Elora stood in front of her, a finger to her lips. The older woman took hold of her arm, helping her stand and then beckoned for her to follow.

Darkness was setting into the forest again as Elora led her to the edge of the clearing furthest from the road. Both their mounts already stood within the trees, tied loosely to a low hanging branch.

Untying them, they went deeper under the shadow of the leaves, trying not to crunch too many of the dry, fallen ones underfoot. It wasn't an easy task.

Elora stopped but still didn't speak; instead, she turned to look back at the road. Matilda stood beside her, desperate to ask what she was afraid of, but she didn't need to.

Over on the road was a small column of cultists, some human, but many of other races. Several marched at the front and back, guarding those in the middle: groups of four, bearing chests, enclosed litters for people, and what appeared to be piles and piles of gold.

Matilda had never seen so much wealth in one place, but she'd also never seen so many guards. There had to be hundreds of them.

They stood watching in silence for at least an hour, the forest growing darker again as the procession continued past them. Eventually, the last guard faded into the distance.

"Come," she said. "My brother-in-law won't dare meet us here after a display like that. The dragon must be living close by. We'll need to find Marl elsewhere."

As before, Matilda couldn't bring herself to ask Elora where they were heading next. The older woman led, and she followed.

CHAPTER EIGHT

Most of another night had passed while Matilda fought to keep her eyes open and stay on her pony. Somehow, she'd managed. They'd not traveled by road this time, Elora taking them alongside it, weaving through the trees. Off to the side of the way, but able to see the dirt track in the dim morning light, they remained hidden from anyone who might happen along.

The sun hadn't yet shown its face when Elora stopped. A frown flitted across her face briefly before she carried on. "There's normally a sentry around here somewhere," she said, falling back enough to whisper to Matilda. "For a small village, Najov. They keep bees and hunt the game nearby and like to keep to themselves. Marl sometimes traded with them for the inn."

"Perhaps they're not awake yet," she replied,

yawning.

"Perhaps…" Elora pushed forward, not sounding convinced by Matilda's suggestion. As they approached a small hut, set against the base of a large tree, she found herself feeling equally concerned. For a village, it was strangely quiet, even at this time of the morning.

"Hello?" Elora called by the door.

No response came but the flapping wings of a bird startled into flight.

"Out hunting already?" Matilda asked, but the words sounded like an excuse, and Elora never deigned to reply.

They carried on, heading to the next dwelling and the next. No one answered Elora's calls. By the time they reached the fifth hut, a much larger building made out of a sturdier wood, Matilda knew something was wrong.

Elora appeared to reach the same conclusion, getting off her horse in front of the building and handing her the reins.

"Wait here. I want to see if I can find out where everyone is."

With no desire to argue, she sat and waited, watching as Elora went up to the wooden door and pushed it open. It swung back on the hinges with no resistance, letting out a waft of steam.

Elora rushed inside, leaving her alone. A few curse words came to Matilda's ears, and the clatter of something metal, and then all was quiet, the wisps of hot air growing less as time passed.

Biting down on her lip, Matilda tried not to panic while she waited. It was still too quiet.

The rush of noise as Elora came outside again made Matilda jump. Before she could exclaim, however, Elora chucked a small piece of stone towards her. Engraved on it were two symbols: fire and a dragon eye.

"The worshipers have been here. Probably taken everyone, just like your camp."

Matilda frowned, not needing to be reminded that they had her parents. *But how many other people had they taken?*

A shiver rippled up her spine as she thought about it.

"I had to take the kettle off the fire, but it hadn't boiled dry yet, and the logs were still burning merrily. They've not been gone long. Let us see if we can find out the direction." Elora said, not waiting for Matilda to answer as she took back her reins and remounted. Within a second, the woman was off again.

This time Matilda was eager to follow. Her parents might be with whoever was taken from this village.

Elora kept looking at the ground as she rode, her head scanning back and forth until she spotted something.

"Horses and wagons came up to here and then moved off again. Led to the road."

Instead of avoiding the dirt track the forest dwellers called a road, Elora now headed towards it, following apparent signs of a large group.

Where the ground was too hard or covered in too

many fallen leaves to see evidence of people passing through, the branches of trees were snapped, and several trunks had been slashed with swords. They weren't afraid of being followed.

As they reached it, Matilda heard the sound of distant voices calling to each other. She also noticed the track had been churned up by hooves and feet. Dust still settling back down again where it had been kicked up into the air by the passage of so many people.

"They can't be far ahead," Elora said, leading her horse that way, but staying close to the edge of the road, out of the worst of the particle-filled air.

Despite knowing the people ahead were likely to be dangerous, Matilda eased her pony forward in the same direction. If following these people helped her find her family, she'd do it. It also beat being alone.

In time, they caught up to the group enough to get the occasional glimpse of the rearmost wagon. There were fewer soldiers and guards than Matilda expected, but she noticed several robed figures, each with the same pair of symbols on the backs of their attire.

Each time they came close to them, Elora slowed her horse until the caravan of people and creatures was out of view again.

"Where do you think they're going?" Matilda asked, as much to make conversation as to satisfy her curiosity.

"I'm hoping they're making for their camp. I want to know how many there are. What resources they have."

"Like a scouting mission?" Matilda let the question tumble out, already picking up on the sudden willingness to divulge information.

"Sort of, although I'm not much of a spy usually. I didn't even believe the stories last time Aldrei was around. I'm not going to let this beast come and claim our land a second time though."

Matilda was surprised by the ice in Elora's voice. Her family had arrived in the area after the last dragon invasion, and she had only heard stories about it. Elora must have lived through it.

As she opened her mouth to ask another question and see if Elora might tell her why she hated the dragon so much, Elora lifted her hand.

Matilda clamped her jaw shut with an audible click. Near silence followed, the only sound the steady clip-clop of their horses' hooves on the ground.

"Thought I heard something," Elora exclaimed a few seconds later as she shook her head. "I guess not. I've been awake too long."

You and me both, Matilda thought.

The morning wore on, mile by mile, until noises up ahead grew louder and more frequent. Many more men were calling out.

"I think we've found them," Elora said as she directed her horse off the road.

With her heart hammering faster at the thought of finding her parents, Matilda tugged the reins on her pony until it matched the pace of Elora's. She had no experience sneaking up on anyone.

They kept back like this for another couple of

hours, listening for the sounds of the group they followed and making sure they could never see them or be seen.

It was a strange way to travel, but Matilda soon adapted, she slowed at the same time as Elora and knew when to urge her pony to pick up the pace. It kept them out of sight.

After a while, they came across the remnants of a stone-built town, an unusually large ruin situated right beside the road. Another dirt track forked off just before it turned in the direction of the Fog. More ruins lined its sides.

Without needing to be told, Matilda steered away from this route. No one went into the Fog. Not if you wanted to come out again.

"This must have been a wonderful place once," she said when they passed the largest building, and she noticed the remains of an ornately carved stone lintel.

"Yes. It was until the Fog came. A bit before your seasons I imagine."

"Not before yours?" Matilda stared at the ruined buildings. Surely these were older than Elora?

But Elora didn't answer. Instead, she frowned and tilted her head to one side.

"I don't think they came this way," she said a moment later. "I can't hear them anymore, and there are no prints in the dirt."

Matilda raised her eyebrows. There had only been one other path—the road into the Fog.

"Then where did they go?"

"I don't know. It doesn't make any sense."

Elora slowed and turned her horse, bringing it about to head back down the road. Copying her actions, Matilda tried not to panic. She didn't want to go into the Fog, not after hearing all the stories.

She didn't doubt some of them were just stories, but equally, a few must have been true. Everyone avoided the Fog. Didn't they?

They hurried back to the junction, but only a few meters before they got there, Elora pulled up her horse and said, "Look. They didn't go down either road, they've come off the path here in the middle. I didn't notice it earlier, but they've gone through the ruins."

Relief flooded through Matilda. They weren't about to go into the Fog on some tracking errand. Or to try and find her parents.

Instead, they picked a path through the moss-covered stones and pathways until they found an almost invisible road of cobblestones.

Time and nature had done their best to reclaim it, covering the road in plants and fallen leaves, but here and there a horseshoe had chipped that away, revealing the cobbles below.

This spot was where the procession had headed. An old road that ran along beside the Fog.

Matilda marveled as they passed by yet more buildings, these more intact than those they had passed before, having been built farther from the forest. Some had roofs or floors still nestled among the sturdy walls. Others had broken remains of furniture visible through windows and open doorways.

As the buildings grew smaller, with larger gaps between them, Matilda noticed the sounds were getting louder ahead.

The pair slowed their mounts once more until it was clear to both of them that they were arriving at some main camp.

"Quick, let's get off the path," Elora said, leading the way past the final ruined wall into the forest again. Just out of sight of the road she stopped. "We'll leave the horses here and get closer on foot."

Matilda obeyed with some reluctance. Her pony was all she had left from her parents.

"Stay safe," she whispered as she tied it alongside Elora's.

"Keep close," Elora said, barely much louder.

Matilda didn't know exactly how near the older woman meant, but she crept in closer.

Each step Elora made was as quiet as possible, avoiding leaves and branches on the ground. Matilda did her best to put her foot on the same spots, hoping not to blunder. Her heart already hammered in her chest and she fought to keep her breathing even. What if they were discovered, or worse?

Closer and closer they got to the camp until they could see tents and people of several different races milling about.

Matilda's mouth fell open as she forgot her fear of being caught. She'd expected to see a temporary camp of slaves and goods, watched over by cultists, but this was far more permanent looking. And there were a lot more people in armor, marching, training, and milling about all around.

While most of the dwellings were canvas tents, it looked like they had been there some time, the grass worn down to mud at the entrance to each, and clotheslines with fresh washing hung between some.

Men took turns firing arrows at targets in a line, and wooden dummies bore the brunt of strikes and blows from would-be duelists. The camp stretched on as far as Matilda could see.

"Hmmm," Elora said a few seconds later.

"Hmmm?"

"Yes, hmmm. There's a lot more of an army than I was expecting."

"You were expecting an army?"

"No. A few soldiers perhaps, as guards, but not an army. This isn't good."

"Why does a dragon need an army?

"Why do you think?"

Opening her mouth to reply, Matilda realized it had been a rhetorical question. It snapped shut again. Silence reigned as they both watched some more.

It was only as she saw some women emerge from a tent with bowls of food that she noticed something remarkable. Everyone here was free. No one was in a cage or kept as a slave.

So where are my parents, and the people from the village?

No sooner had Matilda thought this than Elora stepped away again.

"Stay here; I need to get an idea of the numbers before we go find Marl."

"But what about my parents? The people they

took?"

For a moment Elora didn't reply, pursing her lips together. Matilda could feel her frustration until her expression softened. Elora let out a sigh.

"I'll look for them too, but I make no promises. I can only get so close and still stay hidden."

Matilda nodded. It was enough. As she had remembered these people were some enemy, her heart had begun racing once again, and her mind kept suggesting terrible outcomes of being discovered.

As much as she wanted to find her parents, she also didn't want to become a dragon's dinner herself. Hunkering down behind a bush, Matilda watched Elora creep away.

Crap, she thought, once Elora was out of sight. *I forgot to ask how long she might be.*

But there was nothing she could do about it now. Matilda was alone. Hours passed while she sat, growing thirstier and hungrier. The birds sang overhead, and the camp continued to bustle, different men and creatures coming to train as others grew too exhausted. Matilda couldn't remember the last time she'd seen so many people in one place. And so close to the Fog.

The sound of a twig snapping made her startle. She whipped her head around to look in that direction, but nothing stood there—not even an animal.

"Elora," she said, barely above a whisper.

Wriggling her cramped limbs to get some life into them, she pushed herself into a crouch from where she'd sat. Twice more she repeated the call, but there was no answer, not even from a bird.

Must be imagining things, she thought as she sat back down.

A pointed object digging into her back made it clear she hadn't.

"Stand up slowly," a gruff male voice told her. "And don't try anything."

Matilda hadn't planned on resisting as she got to her feet, hoping it was gradual enough not to earn her a sharp lesson.

"Turn around." The pressure eased on her back, giving her room to move as instructed.

Obeying the command showed her a pair of men, both dressed in the same armor, and bearing the dragon's symbols on shields they carried.

One of them had a set of reins in his hands connected to her pony. She couldn't help herself squealing in surprise.

"This is yours then, I take it?"

She nodded, regaining her senses enough not to let out another sound.

"Come with us then, miss. Our boss is going to want to know why you've been sneaking around our camp." He motioned with his sword for her to move towards the nearest tent.

Biting down on her lip to keep from crying, Matilda let them march her forward. Her only consolation at being caught was knowing her pony was coming along with her.

But finding it alone meant one thing. Elora's horse

had been moved. *Had Elora abandoned her there? Or had something happened to her too?*

CHAPTER NINE

He rode as hard as the horse would go. At the cottage, Callista was sitting by the fire sharpening a curved dagger and singing a soft melody.

The horse had barely stopped, and Marl was off and said, "I've got the stuff for Jenson, where is Raina?"

"She's sleeping, but I'll brew up what we need," Callista said with a nod to a small table with the other ingredients in little piles ready to go. "It will take all night, as the uddeomille needs to be added in incredibly small increments over time to let the potion build to the strength we need."

"Is there anything I can do to help?"

"You could put the horse away. She looks beat. I have everything I need, but after that, if you want to keep me company, it might help pass the time."

Marl didn't mind putting away the horse. At the

stable behind the cottage, he found his horse had been well cared for while he was chasing down the uddeomille. He put away the saddle and tack, filled the trough with some oats and filled the water trough, too.

Taking care of animals was one of the jobs he enjoyed at the inn. He had a boy from the neighbor's farm who worked there, but often he would do it himself, if the bar wasn't too busy. It was his place to think.

He needed to think.

It was clear that Jenson wasn't going to be in any shape to travel, and he couldn't wait for him. Who knew what devastation was being wrought by Aldrei? Who could he get to replace him?

And the more important question, what would it take to defeat an older Aldrei? The last time their party was just enough to drive him away, but it was more a draw than a win. The dragon was still growing into his prime, while Marl was six years further into decline. The battle earlier had shown him how much.

Returning to Callista by the fire, Marl sat down. She continued to hum as she scraped ingredients into the pot.

Marl pointed at her whetstone and asked, "Do you mind?"

She smiled.

He took a seat and began to work on his blade.

Callista stirred the concoction and asked, "Where are you headed from here?"

"I'll probably ride back into town tomorrow and see if I can find a blade to replace Jenson."

"Was he a pretty good fighter, then?"

"He held his own, today. He's alright."

"Gran tells me you're going up against a dragon. Don't you need better than alright?"

"What I need is a miracle."

"It sounds like a dangerous adventure," she said, with a suspiciously casual tone.

Marl looked at her. He knew both her mother and grandmother, and if Callista was half as sneaky, he knew she was driving at something. "I wouldn't call it an adventure. We're not on a quest for a magic bobble. Aldrei is a danger to all that we love."

She smirked. "You sound like my teacher at the archery school. He's a chronically serious man with no imagination."

"You studied archery."

"The game around here has a thing about just wandering up and jumping in Gran's stew."

Marl went back to sharpening his blade.

She added a bit more of her herbs and said something over the pot. A blue flame shot up.

"What just happened?" Marl asked.

"That means we're on the right path. So, how are you going to kill the dragon?"

"Cunning and guile…or more likely luck and prayers. I fear it's grown beyond our means, but I won't know until we find out where it's living. Don't worry about you and your grandmother, I'll do everything in my power to slay the beast or drive it off again."

"I'm not at all worried. This cottage is the safest

place in the world. When you get slaughtered, Gran will just put a spelling of hiding on the place. She'll be fine," She said with a casual certainty.

"Are you a diviner?"

"Yes, but I've not seen your death or anything. You seem to be pretty old for this sort of thing. And, it doesn't sound like you've got much of a plan."

"I'm not as young as I used to be, but there's still a good deal of fight left in these bones. As for a plan, it's not my first battle. I'll suss it out, and we'll be just fine."

"Will you now?"

She said it in a tone that reminded him of his mother when she'd caught him in a lie. He hadn't thought about her in twenty years, but that tone stays with a person, and he cringed a little thinking this barely a woman might be right.

Marl wiped a fingernail across the blade. It was getting there. The fire crackled, and a bat flew overhead, its wings batting against the night air with the familiar thwap, thwap, thwap.

"You want to know what I'd do?"

"By all means, do share with your vast experience on the field of battle and how you'd battle a red dragon. You're sixteen, right?" he said, knowing she was nineteen and feeling it would be a good rebuttal for the old comment.

"I'm nineteen," she said and continued, "You need to start with how you build your party, and you haven't mentioned anything about a healer in your group."

"My sister-in-law will pick up some potions," he

said.

"That's not a great strategy. What happens when the potions run out?"

"I die and don't need to worry about the dragon anymore."

"What you need is someone who's good in a fight and can heal up you and your other old friends."

"You're not coming with us."

"Yes, I am. You need me. I'm great with the bow, and grandmother has taught me more than just healing spells."

"I've never met a mage who could shoot worth a damn."

She stood up, pulled her bow from the ground behind her, and fired three arrows in rapid succession into the top log on a pile of wood at the far side of the property. It was a good shot, and all three landed dead center.

Marl was impressed, but he didn't let her know. "We're not hunting rabbits. Dragons fight back."

"I can cure poison, burns, frost, and magical attacks that render you weak and confused. And then there's my wand. I'm starting to learn a spell that can freeze a human for up to five seconds. It might come in handy."

"You're starting to learn? It sounds like you can't do it. That doesn't fill me with confidence."

"Well, sometimes it works, and sometimes it fails miserably. I've been freezing the stable boy," she said with a laugh.

"He must love you."

"I think he does, which is why he puts up with it. It doesn't hurt him—stops him for a bit."

"Listen, I appreciate your enthusiasm, but you're too young. And I'm not interested in being the one that gets the silver witch's granddaughter killed." His look said it was the final word on the matter.

Callista gave him a dirty look that said it was not the final word on the matter.

They sat without a word for most of the rest of the night. Marl finished with his sword and worked on a couple of knives.

When the potion was close to done, Callista left and returned with her grandmother. "It seems like we've got it, Gran."

Raina took the spoon and dabbed a bit on the palm of her hand. She spoke some words and, using her index finger, swirled the shiny gray concoction in her hand. It glowed for a moment and then hissed for a moment before popping and evaporating into a tiny pale green puff of smoke.

Marl watched with fascination. "And he's meant to drink it?"

The old witch ignored Marl and turned to Callista, "That's a fine potion you've brewed up. It will save his life. Take it to him now, dear."

Raina sat down.

"You're a good woman. Starting with Jenson's death on my conscience wouldn't have been a good sign."

"You have a decision to make, don't you? You'll need to replace Jenson."

"Didn't I just have this conversation with Callista?"

With a laugh, Raina touched her nose and winked. "She's like her mother, who was more like me than I wanted. Probably a punishment from the gods for my wicked ways."

"I didn't think you believed in the gods."

"I do when it's convenient."

"So, I imagine you want to tell me what I should do next?"

"Oh, I'd never presume to tell a fierce warrior like you how to fight a dragon. But you should take Callista with you."

Marl roared. "And what would you do to me if I got your granddaughter killed?"

Raina tilted her head sideways and wrinkled her nose. There was a bit of quiet, and she considered her answer. "Well, I can't give you the specifics of the curse, but it would be both painful and annoying. Plus, I'd make sure it was nigh on impossible to break. I think you'd best bring her back in one piece."

"That's why she's not coming."

The old witch stood up, strode over to Marl, bent down and put her hands on his face. "You need her, and her life journey goes through that dragon. I've seen it. It's destiny, but that doesn't mean you don't need to fight through hell and back to keep her from harm. I'll tell her to pack her bag."

"I said, 'no,'" Marl repeated and stood.

"I can put that curse on you, now, if you prefer."

He stared at the frail-looking woman who seemed

to tower over the argument that he was going to lose. "We'll leave in the morning."

"You're a good boy. Now get some sleep. Saving the kingdom is going to take more than you imagine and twice what you have."

CHAPTER TEN

The cock crowed thrice, but it didn't wake Marl. Raina's scream for the rooster to "shut it," did the trick, though.

Callista was ready. She looked the part of a competent archer. She wore leather armor, her bow over her shoulder, and a look of mocking triumph that was going to grate on Marl's nerves until mid-day.

To her credit, though, she had gotten his horse ready, too. Its mane was brushed, and it was eating an apple. Marl suspected she was making friends, just in case the horse ever got a vote in something.

Marl put it all out of his mind. Their next stop was back to town to find Kal. The first time around, Kal's lightning-fast draw and magic arrows that had a slowing effect were an essential part of their success. His friend had not been to his inn for years, and the word was that the best archer in the land had become a drunk. If this were true, Marl wondered how valuable he would be to the party. Still, he had few options, and there wasn't any way that Callista was going to be an equal substitute.

Marl and Callista didn't talk much as they rode into town to the smithy.

At the Fire and Anvil, a towering man with broad shoulders, dark skin, and eyes black as coal, stopped his hammering and stuck the sword back into the furnace. "Hey there mate, I've not seen you in the capital in ages. What brings you round?"

"I need to find Kal, and if anybody knows where he's tipping pints, it's his best drinking buddy."

"Ah, it's been a while since Kal and I had a lager. We used to be regulars at the Third Eye, but he got pissed, started a fight, and the sisters kicked him out. I went round to see him the next day, and he had gone. Why do you need old Kal?"

"You remember that wyrmling who was causing troubles?"

"Kal has told that story more than anyone wanted to hear it."

"It's back, and it's not a wyrmling anymore," Marl said, the tone in his voice belying his concern.

"Aye, then I best find me a few more hands around this place. It's about to get busy. How's your blade holding up?"

Marl pulled his sword and handed it to the blacksmith. "It's not as good as one of yours, but it gets the job done, Bondor."

Bondor inspected the blade, found the balance

point, and said, "Your man did a fair job, but it could be a faster blade if the weighting were better. I could make you one in four days."

"I don't have four days or enough coin."

"I'll give you a good deal."

Marl held out his hand, and Bondor returned the blade. "Thanks, but we need to find Kal. Any idea where he went?"

"No, but if he's seen anyone since then, it would probably be Vernilla over at the Laughing Clam."

"The what?"

"It's a brothel on the edge of Dark Alleys. Kal never could get his girl."

Callista had been quiet. When she spoke, it was almost as if Marl had forgotten she'd come along. "I know where it is."

Bondor said, "Are you Raina's granddaughter?"

"Yes, sir."

"Tell her my shoulder feels better than it has in years. The balm she whipped up was worth every penny."

"Thanks, I'll let her know," Callista said and turned her horse to leave.

Marl knew it was going to be a long day.

CHAPTER ELEVEN

Marl rode in silence, though he was no longer upset about Callista tagging along. He'd lost his archer, and while she wasn't an equal replacement, she was competent. Along with that, she'd grown on him.

There was something about the exuberance of youth that was infectious. Callista could barely contain her excitement at heading out into the world on an adventure. At her age, life was forever, even if he was leading her to a possible early death.

In the back of Marl's mind, he kept having one thought that gave him solace. The silver witch was a seer, and her insistence made him think that she knew something he did not. It was best to listen to Raina when she gives suggestions, as she was rarely wrong.

The day was hot. The horses needed a break, so they got off at a creek and let them get a drink.

Callista asked, "Why do you think your friend

disappeared?"

"It could be anything, but likely he was moving on. He did that from time to time, usually about three pints after he'd worn out his welcome at his favorite tavern. He had a way of doing that."

"So, he's a drunkard?"

"He's seen some things that would turn you to drink, too. We all have. This adventure you're so excited about may not be all glory and victory. When the tales are told, they always leave out the bits about the friends who died with open bellies and shocked looks."

Callista just gave a knowing nod. "You're right. I need to be more serious. Sorry."

Marl wasn't sure what to say; maybe he'd misjudged her.

They got back on their mounts and headed through the bluffs. Clouds passed overhead and brought with them welcome shadows. Marl thought about his youth. He remembered the first time in battle, how he was pretending to be brave, and how he threw up after pulling his sword from the belly of a man who could have been his younger brother. The first kill never left a person.

But with time, experience, and a little understanding of the reality of life and what must be done to protect those who are loved, Marl came to terms with his life.

He was lost in thought when Callista whispered, "Stop." And without question, he pulled back on the reins and looked at her.

She pointed toward the bluff ahead. "I think I saw a bit of bright blue, maybe the top of a hat. Whatever it was, it's a color that I don't see now."

Marl dismounted and silently drew his sword.

Callista pulled her bow, notched an arrow, and crouched down. The horses just stood there, not moving, sensing there was something amiss.

With his right hand, he pointed to the adjacent bluff, and she understood. Marl crouched down and moved uphill, his muscles ready for action, his heart beating a little faster.

With each step, his eyes scanned from left to right and back. Halfway up the bluff, he saw a bright blue something. A few steps later it was a pointy hat. Then he stood and called out to Callista, "It's okay."

A round-faced man in rather garish garb waved them over. He had a little campsite, a bedroll, and only a few possessions.

"Welcome my friends. I'm so extraordinarily excited to see fellow travelers on their way in the world. It's a glorious day. May I offer you a bit of hot Iberian tea?"

Callista said, "Yes, thank you. I'd love some."

Marl nodded. "Thanks," and then introduced the two of them.

The man's name was Maltise Gato. He described himself as a world traveler and procurer of fine antiquities of the highest order.

Marl looked around. "Did you lose your cart?"

"I did not," replied Maltise, with a sly smile. "These roads are full of folks who, unlike you, may not be trusted. They wouldn't hesitate to bat me on the noggin and ride off with my treasures. I need to be a little cleverer. It's hidden."

Callista sipped her tea. "Well, we're not highway robbers, so you needn't worry. And the tea is lovely. I've never tasted anything like it."

Marl held his cup and brought it to his lips. It was warm, but he had a funny feeling. He'd never heard of Iberian tea, and his late wife adored teas. She knew every type in the kingdoms and talked about her favorites as they lay in bed.

When they were young, poor, and full of unbridled optimism, it was the dreams of travel that they took with them to bed. She wanted to see the known kingdom and then all that was beyond.

Marl knew that the world extended well past the great Fog, but it had been generations and people had forgotten what was out there. The names of the lands were still known to the historians and scholars, but average folks had no need to know about what, for them, didn't exist.

Marl was brought back from his daydream when he noticed Callista giggling to herself.

Maltise looked at Marl and asked, concerned, "Do you not like your tea?"

"Tea was my wife's passion. I'm more of a whiskey drinker."

"Oh well, you're in luck, I've got something I think you might enjoy," he said and went to a little pouch by his bedroll. He stuck his hand in the pouch, well up to the elbow, and pulled out a tiny bottle of something brown. "This is a liquor, which is not exactly whiskey, but I think you'll find much better. It's from a man I know in a small village by the sea. He charges quite a pretty penny for this wonderful elixir. Not only will you enjoy its aroma and flavor, I believe you'll also find it makes those little pains from travel melt away."

"No, thanks, but it's a little early for me."

Maltise frowned. "It's costly, but for my new friends, I'll let you have a taste just to show you proper hospitality." And then he smiled again.

Marl set down his tea. "I'm fine, but that's a generous offer."

Maltise said, "You wouldn't want to offend your host, would you." His voice was stronger than it was before.

"I don't know you, and I think it's best we are moving on, we have a long day."

Callista had laid down and was giggling quietly to herself.

"Get up; we need to get back on the road."

"But it's so beautiful, let's just rest here a bit and watch the dancing flowers on the hill."

"The dancing what?" Marl looked in the direction she was pointing, and all he saw was the grass blowing in the breeze.

Maltise stuck his hand back in the pouch and said, "I have something you might like, Marl, it's a tasty morsel of nuts and berries blended with the famed Alderz Honey. It's exceedingly rare, but if you have just a single copper, I'll give it to you. That's a fair deal, wouldn't you say?" And he pulled out a round wooden box with intricate inlays of bees and flowers. He popped open the lid and tilted the box so Marl could see the goodies inside.

"Callista, stop that."

She was taking off her boots, and her head was weaving back and forth, and she hummed a little song. "Why don't the rocks like the flowers? They hover there and refuse to dance. We should all dance."

Marl was not happy. "Get up now!"

Maltise said, "But wait…"

Marl drew his sword. The speed was shocking, and Maltise's eyes stood wide with terror as the tip of the blade touched his throat. "What did you give her? What's in the tea?"

"Nothing that shouldn't be there. It's just a drink to make you happy and see the world as it should be, not as it is. You really should try it."

"Stop pushing your tea and undo this spell you've put on her."

"It's not a spell; it's just…"

The sword was steady. His voice lowered an octave into an easy tone that carried the weight of a hammer blow from the gods. "Fix her now."

Sweat poured down his face, and Maltise said, "Yes, of course, it's nothing at all. I've got a little potion in my bag here that will make her right as rain." He shoved his arm into the tiny bag up to the shoulder. Maltise seemed to be stretching to grasp something. When he pulled his arm from the bag a silver bottle with a bright blue cork was in his hand. "Here, Callista, take this."

Marl stopped him. He grabbed the bottle, lowered his sword, pulled off the cap, and sniffed the contents. "If this does anything other than put her right, I'm going to run you through and figure it out myself."

Maltise jabbed his hand in the bag, ripped it back out, and the wand he held sparked. A cloud exploded in front of him.

Marl pushed the cork back in the bottle and tossed it toward Callista and dove through the whirling black smoke. On the other side, he was no longer amongst the long grassy berms. A desert stretched out to the horizon. Massive dunes rose to the sky. And on a camel, well off in the distance, Maltise rode.

Behind him, the cloud was beginning to fade. He jumped back through just as it closed.

Callista was sitting up but still looked dazed. The bottle and cork lay on the ground.

"Are you okay?"

"I think so. Where did you go?"

Marl seemed dazed. "I couldn't say. The other side of the cloud was in the desert. I have no idea what sort of sorcery that was, but he was powerful. Are you okay to ride?"

"Let's go. I'll be more careful."

CHAPTER TWELVE

Wexstone was a moderate-sized town north of the Edorian Sea and west of Trentfri. Known for its fishing, weaving, and brothels, the city had grown steadily since well before the Fog set in.

The fishing and trade businesses thrived. Marl wasn't headed there for a good fish stew, though; it was the only place he could remember that Kal had mentioned living. He had told stories on their long rides of a raven-haired beauty who adored him and worked the looms.

It was his only lead.

Callista knew an herbalist in town, and they decided they might stop there first.

At the edge of Wexstone was a tabletop stretch of land where the road was flat and wide. No trees or grass or anything grew from the side of the forest up to the north gate at the city walls. All across this barren stretch were smooth, heavy stones piled on one another to create statues.

Mostly built by children, they were a decoration unlike anything else in the land.

The tradition was, on the first day of summer, the children would take the stones they'd collected over the previous year and find a spot to build their towers. People respected the little creations, and if the wind blew over a stack, one of the city guards would put it back together.

Marl and Callista rode through the field of statues to the front gate. The guards waved them through.

This section of town was where the guards lived and trained. There was an archery range to their right with twenty bays, and each of them were being used. On the left, a man yelled at his trainees as they worked on their swordsmanship. A blacksmith hammered on a piece of plate mail he was repairing, while next door to him, a man sat putting the tips on arrows.

To Marl, it seemed there was more activity than there should be, but it wasn't his concern. He had to find Kal.

An excellent place to start was the fletcher. "Excuse me, I'm looking for a friend of mine, Kal, he's…"

The man held up his hand. "I don't want to know what he's done. That lout owes me for twenty arrows I made special. Picked them up ten days ago, said he had a line on a bit of coin, and if I gave him three days to pay, he'd give me double. And he ain't shown his face in town since. I know, I've been asking around."

Marl asked, "How much does he owe you?"

"These were special arrows. And Kal said he'd pay double."

"I heard you. How much?'

"That rascal owes me ten gold pieces. He said he'd have it and be back..."

This time Marl stopped the man mid-sentence. "Here's five gold. Let's consider his debt paid."

The fletcher looked at the coins, snatched them out of Marl's outstretched hand, and said, "Done, but if you find him, give Kal a knock on the head."

Marl rode off, and Callista followed.

She asked, "Where to next?"

"If I know Kal, and he had some score, we can likely get an idea in the pubs. Once he had his drink, he would get chatty. It was hard to shut him up."

Through the market, with stalls of vegetables, fruit, meats, and sweet snacks, they rode.

On the other side of the market, Callista said, "There's my friend's shop. She always knows what's going on. Maybe she'll have heard something?"

Marl shrugged.

Callista introduced her friend and explained what they knew about Kal.

The woman didn't have much to offer but did know Kal a little. She hadn't seen him since he first got into town but knew that he hung out at the Ox Bow Inn, a tavern down by the docks.

They thanked her and rode on.

The Ox Bow Inn's sign hung at an odd angle. Its chain on the right side had broken, and a rope had been used to hang it back up, but whoever did it, didn't care much for making it look right.

A drunk sat outside, leaning up against the wall. It was the middle of the day, and he was already three sheets to the wind.

Marl said, "I think you'd better stay here and watch the horses."

Callista took the reins of his horse, got off of hers, and then pulled two apples from her saddlebag. Both animals seemed happy with the snack.

Inside the Ox Bow, it was much like Marl's place, except the bar was on the other side of the room and there were a lot of nautical things hanging on the walls. A painting over the bar showed a mighty archer and the nameplate read The Ox Bow.

Only a few customers were drinking at the bar, and a couple sat at a table near the front window. The rotund bartender looked up from sweeping the floor and said, "We've still got some stew from lunch. If you'd like, I could get you a bowl."

"Are the horses safe outside?"

"Yeah. The neighborhood's a little rough, but the guards don't tolerate horse thieves, so nobody will mess with them."

Marl said, "I'll take two bowls and two cups of mead." He went back outside and got Callista.

They sat at a table and ate. The stew was pretty good.

She asked, "Did he tell you anything about Kal?"

"I haven't asked yet. He'll be more helpful after we spend a little coin, and it's been a long ride since we broke camp."

The bartender introduced himself as he set a loaf of bread on the table. "I'm Charlie Crocker; my wee little wife Maggie made the bread. It will be the best you've ever tasted."

Callista said, "It smells wonderful. She must have just taken it out of the oven."

"Aye, she did at that."

With surprising swiftness, Callista produced a knife and sliced off two pieces. She handed one to Marl and then took a bite of hers. All she said was, "Mmmmm, that's amazing."

Marl took his piece and dipped it in the stew. "I'm Marl, I've got an inn up north, and I can tell you I've never served bread like this. Incredible. Could I buy another loaf for the road?"

Charlie's eyes beamed. "Oh, Maggie will be so pleased you enjoyed it. And yes, I'll wrap up a loaf for you," he said and shuffled off through the door to the kitchen.

He took another bite and smiled at Callista. "That was a nice job there."

She looked confused. "A nice job of what?"

"What you said about his wife's bread. It was perfect."

"The bread is delicious."

"You won him over. Why don't you ask about Kal when he comes back?"

Callista tried to hide how pleased she was at the compliment behind another bite of bread. She looked around the inn, studied the walls, and did her best not to look at Marl, who seemed to be enjoying her failed attempt at being casual.

Marl slid a few coins across to her and said, "Tell him he can keep the change before you ask."

"Got it."

Charlie returned with his wife, who truly was a tiny woman. He said, "This is Maggie. She wanted to meet you."

Maggie was grinning from ear to ear as she wiped her hands on her apron. "It's my mum's recipe, God rest her soul, and I'm ever so pleased you enjoyed the bread."

"My mum makes bread, but it's nothing like this," Callista said and handed over the coins to Maggie. "You can keep the change. We've traveled a long way today and sorely needed this in our bellies."

Charlie said, "I'm glad you chose our little pub. Is there anything else I can get you, another round, perhaps?"

Callista tilted her head just a little. "We're fine, but I might like to ask you a question."

"Fire away."

"My friend, Marl, and I are looking for an archer named Kal, but we're having a hard time."

"Oi, I know Kal. I need to be keepin' an eye on him when he's drinking because sometimes he gets a little forgetful about payin'."

Maxine put her arm on her husband's meaty paw and said, "Kal is a good man, but his dreams are bigger than his coin purse. He's always chasing after something that's going to make him rich. Or so he always says."

Marl asked, "Do you know what he's chasing now?"

Charlie pointed over to the wall where a massive map of the realm was hanging. "I can show you about where he went in. Kal and his three mates got word of some treasure in a cave, but it weren't just any cave, it was in a fog."

Maxine shook her head. "Nobody comes back from the Fog."

He patted his wife's hand. "He told me there was a place where the Fog was thinner than most of the rest of it, and he'd be able to see the mouth of the cave from the edge. Right here is where he wanted to go," he said, pointing to a spot.

Marl shook his hand. "Kal's a friend of mine, a good friend, and we've been through some battles together. Does he owe you anything?"

"No, he's all paid up. Gave me three gold coins before he left. I don't know where he picked up them coins, but I'm not one to be poking around in other people's purses if you know what I mean."

A few more minutes of polite chat, another round of telling Maggie how much they enjoyed lunch, and they headed out to see where Kal went into the Fog.

CHAPTER THIRTEEN

The road ran along the bank of fog, not three horse lengths from its depths. It had taken them a day and a half to get there, but they had loaded up on supplies after leaving the Ox Bow Inn.

The night under the stars had been uneventful.

Before investigating the Fog, they set up camp on the far side of the road, back in the trees a bit. Here they tended to the horses and got them settled. Marl worried about going into the Fog, and what would happen to them if they didn't make it back, so he made sure the horses were tied up just at the edge of the trees. If they didn't return, he was confident they would be tended to by passersby and likely stolen.

He hoped they wouldn't be long. A dash into the cave, look around for any signs of Kal and then back out. But one never knows what lies within the Fog.

He wasn't paying attention to Callista when he

noticed her by the edge of the Fog. She had stacked up some wood and covered it in brush. Marl joined her.

She said, "I figured a tiny fire out here might help us when we're in there."

"That's a good idea. Now, get your bow, and let's get ready to take a peek inside."

Callista ran back to the camp across the road, stopped for a moment to pat her horse on the nose and whisper something in its ear, and then darted into the trees. A moment later she was back, bow across her back and her quiver of arrows and a knife on her belt. She carried two torches and sprinted back to Marl.

It was the unbridled enthusiasm that made Marl miss his daughter, but he didn't let it show.

From the forest, they heard birds, but in the Fog, there was only silence. The stillness gave a false sense of confidence. Marl knew not to let his guard down. "Notch an arrow and walk behind me. Keep an eye on our back because in here the danger could come from anywhere."

She did as she was told and said nothing.

He looked up; the sun would set in a couple of turns of the hourglass, so they'd better not dally.

Marl lit one of the torches in the fire Callista had started. He put the other in his belt. They walked like vamp-panthers into the cool mist.

The opening to the cave was small. Marl had to bend down to fit through the hole. The damp musk filled their lungs. Once inside, it opened to a comfortable width, and the walls wound around in a natural arch to the right, straightened out, and then snaked back to the left.

On the cave floor, four sets of footprints were clear. The path split in two. Marl whispered, "The tracks go straight, but I want to head off to the left for just a bit and make sure there isn't anything we don't want to creep up behind us."

Callista's eyes were wide. The adventure was real and the danger palpable.

The path to the left went for a short distance and opened up into a chamber. Someone had lived here once. Crates lined the walls, though the wood was rotted. Two bedrolls lay on the ground, and next to the fire pit were a couple of pans. A stack of a dozen torches sat on the ground, and Marl picked up another one. A layer of dust covered everything. Other than that, there weren't any creatures looming, so they went back to the main path.

Eventually, they came to an opening. The top of the cave stretched into darkness. Their footsteps, even with their trying to be quiet, seemed to echo. It had a vastness to it. Marl watched the footprints he'd been following spread out then come back together.

With the size of this part of the cave, he imagined they had to have a discussion about which direction to search. The four sets of feet headed off along the cave wall to the left.

Marl stopped and whispered. "I don't like this. With this torch, if there's something out there, it can see us, but we won't see any attack until it's too late."

"What should we do?"

"Let's go get the rest of those torches."

When they got back to the pile they had found, Marl had Callista put away her bow and carry the rest of them.

Back at the opening into the main cave, Marl lit one of the new torches and wedged it into a crevice in the wall next to their exit. "Okay, we're going to put a few around here to create a well-lit area, should we need it, to retreat to fight. Creatures that live in caves have good night vision; this will make it a fair fight."

He then moved along the wall to the right and found another spot to wedge a torch. It was ten paces from the first one. Marl walked another eight paces and found another place he could mount a torch. The light from this showed a huge stalagmite coming up from the ground about four paces out. It was the first visible marker he could see in the darkness.

With a hand motion, he directed Callista to head back to the opening. Pointing, he said, "Okay, that gives our battleground a little shape. Set the rest of the torches down and notch up that bow again. We take this nice and slow. You watch my back, and I'll add another five or six torches to this area, then we can continue to follow the tracks. Remember, if we need to fall back, we want to duck back through the gap. If there's more than one attacker, that will limit their options."

"You know your stuff."

"The ones who don't, well, they're not alive."

"Arrow notched. A friend of Gran's does this

great light spell. I wish I'd learned it last time he was visiting."

"That would have been handy, but…" he stopped talking and drew his sword. Tiny feet could be heard scampering in the dark.

It sounded like the creatures were running back and forth directly out in front of them beyond the light of the torches.

Marl said, "Stay next to me by the exit." He lit another torch and lobbed it about ten paces straight into the darkness. The light told the tale.

Hundreds of pairs of little eyes looked at them for an instant and then scampered away. The light also showed a massive pillar with carvings heading up into the darkness.

Marl said, "Do you know what those were?"

"I'm not sure; it was hard to see much."

"Wiglets are tiny fur balls that have a nasty bite, and the tip of their tail is razor sharp. They're easy to kill, but the sheer numbers make them deadly."

"Should we leave?"

"No, we'll be fine as long as we have a torch. You light up a wiglet, and it will panic. Smells awful, though, but then, that gives me an idea." He took another torch, lit it, ran to the spot that the other had landed, tossed the new one about twenty paces.

The scream of wiglets pierced the quiet of the cave. The torch hand landed in the middle of a group of them that weren't quick enough to get out of the way. Their fur went up, and they bolted, fanning the flames, which ignited other wiglets as they ran into them. As the carnage spread, the glow from the creatures gave a brief but complete picture of most of the cave.

There were four pillars which appeared to be on either side of a crevice that ran down the center, and a stone bridge across. It wasn't clear what was on the other side, but at least they knew the layout of the room.

Marl lay another torch on the railing of the stone bridge. He picked up the two he'd thrown. The pillars had spots for torches, so he stuck them in and returned to Callista. The wiglets who caught fire were all dead and smoldering, and the rest had run off.

"I don't know what's on the other side of that bridge, but keep an eye on it as I follow the tracks. We've got six torches up here, and we started with two, so we've got eight left, including the one in my hand. Always track your supplies."

"Got it," she said, her eyes darting back and forth.

The tracks continued along the wall as it curved toward the crevice. When they were just at the edge of the lit areas, Marl lit a new torch, placed the one he'd been using on a boulder, and continued. "This torch will be the first to burn out, but hopefully we will find Kal or what's left of him before that happens."

"Do you think they're still alive?"

"All I know is, there aren't any tracks heading back out of the cave."

The wall curved back, and they came to another path heading out from the main cave. The tracks showed the others had stopped at this opening but then decided to continue along the wall. Marl lit another torch to mark the additional exit, should it be needed. "If we are in retreat, we only duck in here if we don't have any other choice. We don't know what's through there or if it's a dead end."

Callista nodded that she understood.

They came to another large stalagmite that forced them away from the wall, but it had done the same to the tracks, so they were on the right path. When they got back to the wall, the tracks spread out. "It looks like they were spooked by something, they're getting into a battle formation."

A few more paces later, and the tracks were all over the place. There were other tracks, something with big paws. Callista pointed to a spot on the ground, and Marl brought the torch closer. It was blood.

The paw prints seemed to be concentrated in one area, so Marl said, "I think it was just one beast, and it looks like they fought it as a group, but I'm missing a set of tracks." He looked around and found the missing set about six paces off. "Here, this was Kal. He'd have backed off to give himself space to fire. See how he's moved around to the side and behind the beast fighting the others."

Callista bent down and picked up an arrow. "These are finely made. And it's clear from the craftsmanship that these were made by the same fletcher who sold the arrows to Kal."

Marl couldn't help but be impressed. "How can you tell?"

She held up the shaft and pointed to it. "Do you see these three tiny bands?"

"Yes, it's a nice touch."

"It isn't just that, these bands are culver ore. You see how they are slightly raised above the shaft. The fletcher hand carves out the banding and then pours the molten culver ore into the channels. Culver ore cools quickly, but you don't need to know all that, sorry. Culver ore is great at holding magic enhancements. I wonder why he left it behind," she said and then put the arrow in her quiver.

"In the heat of battle, sometimes you're in a bit of a rush," Marl said and held the torch near the ground. "See here; the paw prints are running off. The creature is bleeding, and it looks like at least two of the party chased after it. This set here seems to have some blood spots, too. I think one of them was wounded rather severely. See here, the trailing set, and one leg seems to be dragging."

The paw prints went right up to the crevice and then disappeared.

Callista gasped. "Do you think it leapt across?"

"I can't see the other side. I'd say it made an attempt. Look here, everyone seems to be back in formation, and they're moving along the ravine to the left."

The distance between the cave wall and the drop-off into darkness narrowed until it was the width of a single person. The top of the cave had dropped down to meet them, too. Effectively creating a ledge, they could walk along in single file.

Marl marked the entrance to this narrow passage with another torch.

The light was enough to see that there was what looked like a walkway on the other side, but it seemed to be manmade, more carved out than natural.

On they crept until they found a narrow stone bridge to the other side. This one was much more practical than the first bridge they'd found. It was just a flat walkway without side railings.

Marl scooped up a few loose stones and dropped them off the side. He counted his breaths and waited for the sound of them hitting bottom. Four breaths is a long fall.

Callista said, "That's a deep drop."

"Let's not find out first hand."

When they got back around to where the cave opened up, Marl noticed the tracks turned left and stayed near the wall. "I want to follow the ledge for a bit and see if that beast made it across."

"It would be good to know if it was still out there. It probably needs healing."

Marl stopped. "A wounded beast is twice as dangerous. Never forget that. I doubt it would let you close enough. And from the looks of the fight, the four of them were an even match. We don't want that battle."

"Maybe it's hurt and can't fight?"

Marl decided it wasn't worth the time to argue, and he moved on. "Let's get back to the party's tracks."

Marl continued to mark their path until he was down to his last torch. "Okay, this is the last one. If we don't find something soon, we head back to camp."

"Without finding them?"

"Yes. We don't go blindly into the darkness. There's always another way, even if it means making new torches and trying again."

No sooner had they headed farther into the darkness than they came across a beautifully crafted arch that led to a hall with intricate tile work along the floor.

"What is this place?" Callista asked.

"I don't know, but it seems Kal was right, this is where one would find the sort of treasure that sets one up for a lifetime…or ends it."

The hall had other arches that led to rooms or other halls. The layer of fine dust on the floor made it easy to follow Kal's party.

A few times the set of tracks of the injured man seemed to show he had stopped to rest. The further the tracks went into the main hall, the more they became spread out, with the injured man lagging.

"They're not staying together. Stupid," Marl said disgustedly. "Kal always did rush into danger without thinking."

Then, suddenly the tracks from the injured man just stopped. Nobody was found in a pool of blood, just a step up to a pile of rubble and tiles, and then nothing more.

Marl said, "Keep sharp. I don't know what happened, but I don't like the looks of it." He peered up and saw a broken-out spot in the ceiling. "Damn it, something was hunting them, and I don't think it was the panther."

Callista pulled her pair of gloves from her waistband. She took a step up on to the pile of rubble, reached to the edge of the opening and pulled down some spider silk. She showed it to Marl. "Don't touch it without gloves."

"Do you know the type of spider?"

She held it close to his nose. "That sweet smell is the acid that covers the silk. This is a dread fire spider."

Marl wasn't happy. "They are not something we can tangle with, just the two of us. If we see one, there will be others. The silk burns well, so I'll try to light it up, and then we run."

"What about Kal?"

"If we see a spider before we find him, then he's out of luck and likely dead. We run. Got it!"

She didn't answer but nodded.

"I think we're better off with torches than weapons. They don't like fire and are too tough to kill with a shot or two from your bow or with my sword," Marl said as he sheathed his weapon.

Callista put the arrow back in the quiver, slung the bow over her shoulder, and pulled out two torches. Marl lit them and a second one for himself.

About five paces farther on, all the tracks seemed to come together in a group, then there were a couple of steps that headed back to where they had started, turned back around, and they all headed off again.

This time the footprints were in a tight line, and it was clear the last set kept checking behind them.

The hall turned to the right, went down some stairs and opened into a vast room, completely covered in dread fire silk. The stench of decay hung in the hair, along with three bodies.

Marl said, "Don't touch the silk."

"I know."

"Good," he said and moved closer to the cocoons around the bodies. The first two were in pretty bad shape. Marl turned to the third one, set one of the torches down, pulled out his knife and poked at the legs. A tiny muffled voice cried out.

"Kal is that you?"

"Help me."

With the knife, he cut the cocoon down, and it fell to the ground with a thud. Marl didn't hesitate, he tossed the torch into the room, bent over, slung his friend up over his shoulder, the acid from the silk burned his hands. He said, "Run."

They bolted up the stairs. The flames consumed the silk and put off great billowy smoke which filled the giant room. From the ceiling, spiders dropped to the ground. Chittering noises were right behind them.

Above, on the ceiling of the hall, more padding feet were in pursuit.

Callista stopped at the hole where the other person had disappeared and lobbed one of her two torches into the tunnel above. Silk burst into flame.

Marl had to slow because she had the light.

Callista ran smoothly and steadily. Just far enough ahead that Marl wouldn't lose the light. She reached the edge of the crevice and stopped. Marl caught up.

"Go, what are you waiting for?"

"This way," she said, bolting to the left instead of the way they came.

"No, where are you going?" he yelled at her, but it was too late, she was in full sprint.

There weren't any options; he had to follow.

A terrible scream sounded from the hall they'd just left. The spiders were gaining on them.

When he caught up with Callista, she was at the four pillars and the bridge. The torch lay on the ground, her bow was out, and she scanned the darkness.

His chest pounded, lungs burned, and sweat poured down Marl's face.

"Don't stop."

Marl ran past her over the bridge, and she fired an arrow dropping a smaller spider that was right on his heels. Then another shot, but this shot only slowed the much larger spider that now closed on the bridge.

She reached down and grabbed the torch, backed up on the bridge to the mid-point and set it back down on the side rail.

Marl yelled, "Come on, we need to leave."

From the darkness, all around, hundreds of spiders were converging on the bridge. Their chatter grew like a rumble of rolling thunder. They must have numbered in the hundreds.

The wounded spider, much larger than the one she'd killed, stopped at the edge of the bridge and leaned its head back. A stream of web silk spewed forth to the center of the bridge. Like a blanket flying through the air, it would cover a third of the span. Callista loosed an arrow and hit the beast clean through the eye. It fell.

The webbing, still connected, arched down upon her. Like a cat, she flipped backward in the air, spun, rolled on the ground, and leapt forward out of the path. The web dropped onto the bridge and the torch that rested on the railing and burst into flame. The smoke cloud rose.

Marl had set down Kal, drawn his sword, and then realized her plan. As she got to him, Kal was back on his shoulder, and they both flew through the cave and out into the Fog.

It was thick, disorienting, and eerie in the calmness. A faint glow off in the distance showed the way. Marl made for the glow, slowing his run to a walk. Callista trailed behind him walking backward, bow at the ready, and then they were back to the fire.

Marl lowered Kal to the ground, his hands burning. "Can you cut him out?"

Callista drew her dagger and carefully cut away the silk around Kal's face. His arms were trapped by his side, but he had gotten his gloved hands in front of his face before the spider had finished the cocoon. As soon as she pulled back the silk, his hands parted, and he smiled.

"Hey, love, I'm Kal. Thanks for getting me out of that rather sticky situation. The old girl back there and I didn't get along...so, are you single?"

"Maybe I'll just cut away the rest of it tomorrow."

"Oh, don't be like that."

Marl said, through clenched teeth, "Leave her be, Kal, or I'll chuck you back in the cave myself."

Callista left Kal lying on the ground. She ran across the road to where they had tied up the horses. From her saddlebag, she pulled a dark red bulbous bottle with a silver cork and ran back.

Kneeling by Marl, who had laid down next to the fire and was still panting and out of breath, she said, "Give me your hands."

Eyes closed, he raised both arms.

"This will heal you up in an hour or so, and it will take away the pain. That fire silk is nasty stuff," she said as she took a dab of the liquid to spread on his hands.

She covered the back and front of each hand, then applied a second coat, to be sure, and said, "Try not to do anything with your hands while I tend to Kal. The balm will dry soon. You don't want any of it to come off until it does."

When she returned to Kal, she said, "Okay, I'll cut you out of here."

"You have any water?" he asked.

She ran back to the horses and returned with two water skins.

"How long have you been in there?"

"I don't have any idea. Long enough that Mrs. Fuzzy Legs made a right fancy feast out of my mates."

Callista frowned. "Here, take a sip of water," she said and poured a mouthful. "I'm going to peel back the silk from your head, but this may hurt. It doesn't look like you were wearing anything."

"Nope, and I see the error of that decision, now."

She cut a slice and with gloved hand peeled back a tiny section just above his hands. The forehead was bright red and badly burned.

"How does it look?"

"Well, you'll want to wear a hat next time you're chatting up the ladies."

"That bad?"

"I was sugar coating it a little, to spare your feelings," she said and then poured some water over the area. "This is going to take a while. I'll be right back; I've got something for the pain."

"Oh, I've gotten used to the pain."

"No, not that pain; what is to come."

"More sugar coating?"

"Sadly, yes."

Kal didn't answer. She had found the limits of his joy.

Callista brought back the other two water skins and a bottle of deep blue liquid. She poured a mouthful into Kal and then did the same for Marl, who remained lying there with his hands in the air.

Then, with slow precision, she cut away the rest of the silk from Kal's head, washed the scalp, and applied the balm. He winced a couple of times, and she gave him another dose of the healing potion.

By the time she'd finished with Kal from the neck up, Marl was on his feet. "You're quite the healer."

Callista grinned. "Gran is a good teacher. It's been long enough that you can rub your hands together, and the dried balm will fall away."

He looked at his hands with astonishment. "It's like they're good as new. Better, in fact, the bump on the back of my hand is gone." He flexed his finger and made a fist. "Maybe we should move Kal over to the camp."

"Put on gloves," she said matter of factly.

Back in the forest where they had the rest of their gear, Marl propped Kal up against a tree and went to gather wood and to find a place to fill the two water skins, which were now empty.

Callista poured a full water-skin over the thread covering Kal's shoulders. She picked up a branch, broke off a piece about the thickness of her thumb and peeled away the bark.

"What's that for?" Kal asked.

"The silk."

He looked confused.

"Don't you know what this is worth?"

Kal looked confused.

"I'm going to unravel you the rest of the way. First, though, I need to wash off the fire acid. It will take a long time, but you need to rest anyway, so I'm going to salvage it."

She went to work. With the precision of a master craftsman, she washed and unwound the thread. As it came off clean, she wrapped it around the makeshift spool. The sun was setting when she finally had Kal released from the cocoon.

The spool was thick with the now clean spider silk. Callista poured water over it. She wrapped it in a small animal skin she'd pulled from her saddlebag.

Marl had found a stream deeper in the forest and had filled up the water skins several times. He'd hunted a bit of game and, by the time she'd finished, had dinner ready.

Having not eaten in some time, Kal was literally starving. He tore off a bite and ate it. After a few more, he laid his knife down and just stared off into space.

Callista knelt beside him and cut off pieces for him.

The bravado was gone.

Staring into death and moving past the point of acceptance does that to a person. "Thanks for…"

"Quiet. That healing potion will fix you up, and the balm needs to do its work, but you need to rest."

Marl just watched. *Was this what the silver witch had seen?*

The stars shone through the breaks in the canopy. Marl tended to the horses and refilled the water skins one more time. With everyone fed, he suggested Callista get some sleep, and he'd keep an eye on things. She didn't object.

He kept the fire going as the night wore on. Marl thought about the last time he'd been sitting in a field with adventurers after their triumph against Aldrei, and then his mind, as it always did, moved forward to the next day when he found his family.

With no small amount of effort, he put it out of his thoughts. There was work that needed to be done. He needed to get them on the move, as he was sure his sister-in-law was already at their meeting spot.

If they didn't get there soon, she'd head off to find him. She had always been impatient, and he couldn't imagine where Elora might head. Time seemed to be screaming at him, *Get going, Aldrei grows stronger.*

Marl put away his sword, which he'd kept at the ready, and was asleep as soon as he lay down. Who knew what the new day would bring?

CHAPTER FOURTEEN

Kal was the first up. The sun was still sleeping, and the creatures of the woods hadn't begun their pre-dawn warbling. He tended to the fire and let Marl and Callista sleep.

The urge to run his hand over his scarred scalp was one he was fighting. He'd never been the most handsome guy in the bar, but he'd been good enough to spend the cold nights wrapped in someone else's arms. Would he frighten them all off, now?

As he wandered off through the dark of the forest with only a vague idea of where Marl had gone to refill the water. He chastised himself for heading into the unknown of the cave without being more careful.

How many times had Marl warned him about the dangers of running into situations blindly?

Kal tripped over a branch and hit the ground with a thud.

The face-plant stung a little, as he only partially caught himself on the way down. A bush had snagged his right arm.

Rolling over, he spit out a leaf from the forest floor. Undaunted, he patted around until he found the water skin. There was a little water left in the one he'd dropped, so he washed out his mouth and continued in the direction he assumed was the river

If he had only taken his time, paid attention to the hall they had hurried down, he would have noticed the hole in the ceiling. Even a brand-new adventurer would have seen the spider silk and rethought their plan. But no, he had to hurry. He was always in a rush.

A limb from a tree smacked him in the forehead. The forest was pitch black, and he could barely see enough to move through the undergrowth.

Why didn't he listen?

What was it about his stubbornness to not take advice from people he trusted? It made sense, not to head off into a battle, or cave, or ruin without first having a plan. Why did he continuously assume everything would be all right and stumble blindly into one problem after another?

A thorn bush snagged his leg and held Kal up while he cut his way free. There were a few scratches, but compared to the burning of the acid from the silk, it was nothing.

Kal drank the last of the water and was ready to find the river.

He stopped for a moment. There was little sound, but he heard what he needed. Running water was just ahead.

With the machete he'd borrowed from Marl, he cut his way through a particularly dense patch and found himself staring at a clump of large boulders. A few minutes of hacking, and he worked his way around the rocks.

The more he thought about the spiders, the more he became determined never to wander off into the unknown again.

Kal didn't notice he'd reached the edge of the riverbank. It was muddy. His feet flew out from under him. Into the water, he went. It was deeper than he imagined.

Losing his footing sent him into the torrent of rushing water at an odd angle. It took a moment because he was holding on tight to the water skin in his hand, but he got righted. A few leg kicks and a poor excuse for swimming found him on a sand bar at the edge of the river.

Well, it wasn't how he planned to get the water, but here he was. Since he was already lying on his back, he rolled over, opened the water skin and held it in the cold current. When it was full, he replaced the cap, pulled the second skin off his shoulder and filled it.

The forest canopy opened up over the river, and he could see the first signs of daylight.

Without thinking about it, he wiped his hand across his forehead covered in sand and mud. It was the most fantastic thing; his skin wasn't as he imagined. It was smooth to the touch.

He ran his hand over the top of his head. All the hair was gone, but the scarring was, too. It had burned so badly when he was in the silk, he had pictured that if he survived, he would have a terrible looking head where his beautiful hair had once been.

Kal leaped to his feet. He would not be a hideous mess that never knew the soft touch of a woman. He was back.

As he looked around, there was only one problem: which way to camp?

It was not light enough yet to tell which way the dawn was breaking. He considered just sitting on a log and waiting until he could see shadows, and then he would be able to find his way back. This thought didn't last long. Kal brushed some river muck off his legs and headed back into the brush. He'd lost the machete.

When he'd spent more time walking out then he figured was right, he stopped. The sun was now high enough he could get his bearing. To his dismay, he'd gone the wrong way. The camp was not only in the exact opposite direction, but it was also on the other side of the river.

When he made it back to camp, Marl had breakfast ready and wore a knowing expression that was a cross between disgust and resignation.

Callista sat crossed legged on the ground. She had been busy, too. In front of her was a pile of herbs, flowers, and mushrooms. She smiled at Kal. "We were going to give you until we finished breaking the fast before Marl was going to teach me how to 'track a forest idiot.'"

Kal laughed. "We are a rare breed, but highly prized."

Handing Kal a plate, Marl asked, "Where did you go?"

Held high above his head like a great trophy, he said, "I've filled up the water skins. Admittedly, I drank most of the second one finding my way back out of the forest, but there's still one full and half of the other."

"Well, I can't say you're not contributing."

"I'm nothing if not a team player, mate. So, were you passing by, decided to duck through the Fog into the cave, and happened across my secret resting spot, or were you looking for me?"

"It's back."

"What's back?" Kal asked taking a bite of his food.

"The wyrmling, Aldrei."

"And you're getting the band of misfits back together?"

"In a manner of speaking, yes."

"Who have you found?"

Marl ate a few bites. "Gerald wasn't able to come, so he sent his boy Jenson."

"And, where is he?"

"We ran into some thugs, had a scrap, and he's recovering at the silver witch's place. Which is where I picked up this stray," he said pointing his knife at Callista.

Kal said with a huge grin, rubbing the top of his

head, "I'm glad you did. I was sure I was going to be uglier than a dread forest troll after that fire silk. But it looks like your magic balm put me right back to my normal handsome self."

Callista tilted her head. "I guess you old folks use that word differently than we do. But you're welcome, and it's nice to meet you." She returned to her sorting with a slight smile and a wink at Kal.

Both men roared.

When the laughter died down, Kal asked, "What of Elora?"

"She had to warn some of her people down around Ranskill. I think she was going to swing through Wexstone, Cander, and then meet up between Antwick and the capital. You remember the spot?"

"I do. So, we'll be headed there, next?"

"That's the plan. Elora will box both our ears for being late, but it couldn't be helped. Tracking you down was harder than I figured. And what were you trying to find in the cave?"

Kal got that look on his face that Marl hated.

Marl shook his head. "Don't even say it."

"It's funny you mention our old friend the Northern Red. He's going to be a far site bigger, now, and I'd think he's got his breath."

"Let me guess; you just happened to be trying to find some magic item we can't live without. No doubt you got this tip from someone you just happened to run into, and it only cost you a couple of coins?"

"It wasn't at all like that," Kal said, feigning offense, and then continued, "Well, it wasn't exactly like that."

Marl's blank expression spoke volumes.

Callista had stopped sorting, and from her expression, she was enjoying the show.

"You see, it's like this, I was having a drink with a lovely gentleman who was down on his luck…"

"Stop. You've fallen for that line more times than I can count."

The back and forth picked up. Both men got louder, volleying back stories and rebuttals at a blinding pace. It was outstanding theater.

Marl stood and said, "And what about that red-headed thief at the inn in Karvani who had a protection ring she'd let you have, if you just helped her get back that rare knife cruelly taken by the merchant on the edge of town."

"Okay, I'll admit, that didn't go as planned, but in my defense, she was an excellent kisser, and she had really big…" he stopped, looked at Callista and finished, "…hands. And I thought she might be someone who could handle a sword."

"Leave your sword out of this. You got suckered."

"I wonder what ever happened to her."

Marl turned to Callista. "We leave in thirty minutes."

"Hold on, and I never told you what were we after."

"I don't care."

Callista asked, "What was it? I'd like to know the end of the story."

Kal began waving his hands. "The greatest artifact

we could ever hope to find. It's worth a fortune. My buddy told me that in the very cave you found me, the great wizard McAllister the Swift, who disappeared into the Fog fifty years ago, had died. Do you know what sort of kit he had?"

"I've never even heard of him," she said, and turned to Marl, "Have you?"

Marl shrugged. "Yes, there was a powerful mage, and he did disappear fifty years ago."

Kal jumped to his feet. "He was known for having three ancient artifacts, the Quicksilver Cloak, Ramian's Boots, and the Beast Summoner Staff. Any one of them is worth a castle keep."

Marl had finished off the stew and was cleaning up. "So, why would your drinking buddy sell you this King's ransom's worth of treasure for a few coins?"

"Even if it is a wild goose chase, the gear my departed mates traveled with was an upgrade from that ancient armor you're wearing. And there were a couple of nice-looking chests near where you found me hanging. If Aldrei is truly back, and six years older, we'll need to upgrade everything. And one of my mates had a brilliant long sword that Elora would wield like a master. It's the least you can do, making her wait and all."

Callista said, "I know I am new to this, but we've already got a pretty good understanding of what we're up against in there. How many of the spiders are already dead from the fire?"

"I told you, Callista, that these spiders were too much."

"Yes, but that was the two of us, now we have Kal."

"Kal doesn't have a bow."

"He can use mine. I'll be fine with my daggers. What's the harm in taking a peek?"

Marl let out a sigh.

"We do it my way. I'm in charge," Marl said with resignation.

"Good man," Kal said and turned to Callista, "Now, let's take a look at that bow of yours."

CHAPTER FIFTEEN

Marl said, "Well, let's get prepared."

Everyone got to work. Kal spent some time practicing with Callista's bow, while Callista made up more torches so that they could light their movements through the cave. Marl, who was still grousing about the whole idea, tore apart a shirt to make some bandanas to cover their faces, and he wrapped his hands before making sure to put on his riding gloves.

When they were ready to go, Callista spread her balm on the few exposed parts of their skin. She'd explained that if anyone got hit with fire silk, the lotion wouldn't stop the burning, but it would immediately begin countering it and make the sting much less painful.

Marl reiterated that he was in charge and Kal promised not to run off. Their plan was to see how many spiders were left and, if the numbers were manageable, to retrieve the gear from Kal's fallen friends. Only then would the decision be made about continuing the search for supposed artifacts.

They made their way to the gap that led to the main room. An acrid smell of burnt spiders filled their nostrils. Callista coughed for a few seconds, but nothing came at them from the shadows.

There wasn't any need to take the same route, now that they had learned the bridge led to the same place. Marl and Kal quickly lit up the area just before the bridge. This spot would be their fallback position. Before heading to the spot where they knew the bodies, now likely charred, would be hanging, they lit up the rest of the area around the four pillars.

What they found were two more halls leading off. Marl didn't like the way things were shaping up. If another threat lived down either hall, then regardless of where they went next, it was possible to get flanked. Kal had to use his charm to keep Marl from quitting right then and there.

They decided to go back to where the bodies would be and assess the threat.

The hall outside the room where Kal had been hanging had a couple of large dead spiders on the floor. It seemed they had caught fire and fled the burning web, only to die anyway.

At the entry to the room, the overpowering stench of dead spider and burned corpse made it hard to go on. The walls were covered in soot. On the floor, the bodies of Kal's mates. Nothing could be heard, and there wasn't any sign of new webbing.

Kal checked the bodies and found most of the armor severely burned. He found a couple of coin purses, two nice rings, a jeweled dagger and sword, which he gave to Callista.

"I've not trained with anything but a short sword, but this is better than the daggers. Thanks."

Marl continued to scan the room. Just as Kal had said, there were two chests in the corner and another smaller one on a table. They had been covered in webbing and were pretty well charred, but none had come open. The little chest had a handful of pearls, two rings, and an amulet. It wasn't clear if they had magical properties or not, but regardless they would fetch a nice bit of coin.

The two larger chests were locked. Kal made quick work of the locks. Before he opened the first one, he said, "This is it, I can feel it."

Marl shook his head. "You think that McCallister died in here but before he did, put his most valuable artifacts in the chests?"

Callista asked, "Wouldn't those be still on his body? The spiders wouldn't have any need of them."

Kal shrugged. "You're right. Well, let's see what we've got."

The first one contained five scrolls and a coin purse, well, actually two purses. "That's not a bad haul if I do say so myself."

The second chest had a gorgeous dress, two pairs of shoes, and a necklace. "Well, that was a bust," Kal said.

Callista held up the dress and said, "This is lovely.

Look at the stitching, and the bodice, a master seamstress made this dress. And the shoes, those are for feet going to a fine ball." She pulled them out, and packed it away in the bag she'd brought, carefully folded the dress, and tossed the necklace to Kal. "I'd say these are worth a few coins."

"You keep them; they'll look good on you when you attend that fancy dress ball."

At the back of the room, Marl investigated a door revealed when the webbing burned away. "Kal, can you open this? It's locked."

The door was massive and heavy. The lock system had Kal stumped, and he broke his lock pick. "Damn, that was my last one."

"Since when do you run of out lock picks?" Marl asked.

"I've been a little low on gold of late. Not much copper or silver, either."

"You didn't think you might need them when you set out for this cave?"

"Honestly, I thought we'd find the wizard and be done with it. The plan was to get in and get out. None of us wanted to stay in the Fog for long."

Marl understood and stopped giving his friend grief. "Speaking of which, since we can't get through the door, let's call it a day and get out of here."

Kal protested, but this time Callista sided with Marl and suggested they'd done alright. She pointed out that they could always return, the cave and the Fog weren't going anywhere.

They didn't dally.

Marl broke into a light jog, and the others followed. It took little time to get back into the Fog. The signal fire, which Callista had started before they entered, made finding their way out a breeze.

The horses grazed.

Before they had gone into the cave, they had packed up most of their gear. A few minutes later, it was time to mount up.

Kal suggested Callista ride behind him.

Callista said, "It's my horse. You can ride behind me or walk."

Marl laughed. "Don't look at me, and I'd make you run along behind. You are so fond of running off."

They decided to head back to Whitvale, where they could find a room and a stable for the horses. It was about a forty-kilometer ride, which they should be able to do without pushing the horses too hard.

From there, Marl would try to figure out their next move. He imagined that Elora might have left their meeting spot. She was not especially patient, but the question was, where would she go?

The most likely place was Trentfri. If Marl assumed this is where he would find her, he could send a bird ahead with a message that they were on their way and that he could get to the silver witch's place in seven days. Chasing down Kal had taken much longer than he had hoped, but they had him now, so she would be happy to hear it.

When they reached Whitvale, it was dark.

The stable boy took the horses.

Kal was a silver-tongued haggler and was able to

trade the necklace and twenty gold coins for a young mare. An extra five gold got him the saddle and tack. There wasn't anyone who could tell him the value of the rings or what they did. He counted up their remaining coins, and they had one hundred and twenty gold left, which he divided up.

At dinner, Kal gave Marl and Callista their gold.

Callista had never had forty gold all to herself. She held the purse in her hand for a long while and just kept bouncing it up and down in her hand.

With a knowing look, Marl said, "Well, that's it, she's done. It's a life of chasing rumors and fighting beasts for this one. She's good with a bow, but still has a lot to learn."

Callista tucked the coin purse away and asked Kal, "Will you teach me?"

"Of course, I'd be happy to. If we cut across to Cander, they have a decent fletcher, so that I can pick up a bow and some practice arrows. Let me see your arms."

Callista pushed up her sleeves.

"You'll need to put on some muscle if you want to use more powerful bows."

She looked at her arms. "I'm stronger than I look."

Kal smiled in a way that made her nervous. "We'll see."

CHAPTER SIXTEEN

They left early. It was possible to get to Cander in two days, but they would be long days. Kal wanted to push especially hard on the first day, so they could get into Cander the next day before the shops closed.

By switching between walking and trotting, they made good time and rode well into the night. When they reached the point on their map that Kal thought was far enough, they made camp. Nobody had the energy to do much more than care for the horses and eat the jerky and bread they'd bought that morning.

The next day was miserable in the morning. Rain started about an hour after they had broken camp. It was a slow, steady rain that didn't let up until well after lunch. Marl and Kal seemed to be suffering more than Callista.

Marl said, "I'm getting too old for this."

Kal laughed. "You and me both, my friend. Still,

wet in the saddle is better than hanging in that spider's lair."

"I think the rain is nice," Callista said, with a youthful exuberance which was not at all appreciated by the others.

The land between Whitvale and Cander ran between the thick forest and the Black Spire Mountains. It was probably safer to travel south to Wexstone and then along the coast and up the river to Cander, but that would add three days to the journey, and they didn't have the time.

Few travelers like to ride through the shadows of the Black Spires, a small range that seemed to jut up from the earth and looked out of place. The midnight-black granite and razor-sharp peaks were stunning to view. The rumors of dark creatures calling it home kept even the hardiest adventurers away. Some thought the mountains haunted.

By mid-day, though, they had put the mountains behind them and were only about four hours from Cander. Kal figured, if they went back to walking and trotting, they could shave some time and guarantee they would get to William's Bows before he closed up for the night.

It had been a difficult two-day ride. Marl took the horses to the stables, while Kal and Callista made their way past the market stalls to the little archery range in the middle of town. William's Bows was a family business that had been making the finest stringed weapons and arrows in the land for three hundred years.

Kal said, "The bows here will make your head spin. Some of them cost thousands of gold."

"How could a bow be that expensive?"

"Magic, but don't you worry about that, your bow is fine. I'll pick up a cheap longbow, some arrows, and a quiver, and we'll be set. I do want you to try out a few of the bows, though, as you'll soon need to upgrade."

"Why?"

"Because while your bow is great for hunting, it doesn't have the power you'll need against armed men or dragons. And one more thing: let me do the talking."

"No problem, old man."

Kal looked at her sideways before opening the door to the shop.

A young man with reddish-brown hair stood behind the counter. "Welcome to William's Bows. How can I help you today?"

"I'd like to see your longbows."

"We've got a fine selection," he said, and led them to a rack near the stairs to the second level.

Kal had a good eye. He ran his finger along a bow and asked, "Is this Ipe wood?"

"It's mostly Ipe, but it's backed with bamboo. It's lightweight but incredibly sturdy. You'll find its accuracy at range is excellent. Would you like to test it?"

"Yes, thank you."

The young man led them through a door into the back room. Three craftsmen didn't look up from their benches as they walked through to the range behind the shop. When the shop had first been built, it had been on the edge of town, but Cander had grown around them. Still, they had six shooting lanes: two each of 25-meters, 75-meters, and 150-meters in length.

Each lane had a bundle of arrows. Kal went to the 75-meter lane and nocked an arrow. He loosed it in a low arc to the target. It made a resounding "thwack" as it landed in the nine ring.

Callista was impressed.

Kal pulled three arrows from the bundle. He held them in his right hand by the ends, looked at Callista, and then back at the target. With the grace of a monk practicing their martial arts, he fired each of the three arrows one after another. The third was on its way before the first one hit.

All three were in the ten ring.

Without looking back, and with a practiced casualness, Kal moved to the 150-meter range. He pulled three more arrows, aimed higher and sent all three into the center, again.

The young man and Callista looked at each other.

Kal said, "How much?"

"It's a hundred twenty gold," the clerk said, still taken aback by Kal's mastery.

Kal pulled one of the rings from his pocket. He'd polished it while riding, and it shone bright gold with a ruby in the center.

The clerk looked at the ring and assessed its value at one hundred and twenty, but Kal wasn't having any of it. They negotiated and finally settled on one hundred and eighty, which gave him enough to buy sixty of the best-quality non-magical arrows and five arrows with a freezing bonus. The clerk threw in two quivers and ten practice arrows, and the deal was done.

Before they left, Kal pulled a bow from a rack and handed it to Callista. "This will be your next bow. Give it a pull."

She took the bow and tried to draw it back but failed. "Okay, I get it, I need to be stronger," she said with a resigned look.

Kal nodded. They thanked the clerk and headed to the inn where they were to meet Marl.

Exhausted from the ride, Marl suggested they sleep in a little the next day, and everyone agreed it was a good idea.

When the cock crowed, however, Kal was standing at the edge of Callista's bed. He had nine of the practice arrows in his right hand and one in his left. With it, he poked Callista.

She shot up with a fright. "Oh, it's you," she said, and rubbed her eyes. The first golden light of the morn shone through the tiny window of her room. A glint of light caught the arrowheads in Kal's hand.

"Get up. It's time to practice."

"I thought we were sleeping in."

Kal thwacked her leg with the arrow, turned for the door, and said, "Be downstairs in five minutes, or your first day of training will be much longer than I'd planned."

As soon as he was gone, she swung her legs out

of bed, grabbed her pants, and got dressed. She used a short piece of cord to hold her hair in a ponytail, buttoned up her shirt, and put on her boots. The dreariness of sleep still hung in her head, but she wasn't going to let Kal give her a hard time for being late, and so she bounded down the stairs and out the door into the fragrant morning air.

"That was quick. Well done. Now, take these and fill them up," he said, handing her two buckets.

Callista took them and started for the well at the edge of the property.

Kal made a clicking noise with his mouth.

She looked back.

"Not the well, the river."

"But it's all the way on the edge of town," she said, not sure she believed him.

Kal pulled a knife from his belt, drew a line in the dirt, and stuck the knife in the ground. "Be back with the water before the shadow reaches the line."

She looked down. It was clear it wouldn't be but ten minutes. Callista liked a challenge and wasn't about to lose in this game. She took off like a bolt. Through the streets, past the market, turned at the main road and headed for the gate.

The river was just outside the wall.

The bank was dry. Callista hopped down to the water's edge, scooped the first bucket into the icy stream, and set it down to grab the second. The moment she had the second one filled, she whirled around, ran back up the bank, and sprinted to the gate.

The guards watched with amusement. "What's the

rush, lassie?"

She breezed past them and sprinted down the empty morning street. The waters sloshed as she ran, but she set them down, still mostly full, next to the knife with just a sliver of space left between the shadow and the line. "Ha, I did it."

Kal was putting a log on the fire. A large black kettle rested over the flames. "Okay, in here with it then."

Triumphantly, she poured the water into the kettle and set the buckets down.

Kal picked up the knife, looked at the blade a moment and then flicked it into the ground. "Well, you better get going. The sun isn't going to wait for you."

"Again?" She asked, still gasping.

"Until the kettle is full."

"Fine," she said defiantly, grabbed the buckets and off she went.

The guards smiled and watched. They made several not so helpful comments as she returned with the second round of water. This time the enthusiasm for the challenge was gone, and the muscles in her shoulders were starting to feel it.

Kal was whittling on a branch when she got back.

Callista didn't say a word. She dumped the water in the kettle and took off again, even before he had a chance to reset his crude sundial. Her lungs burned a little, but she figured two more trips, and she'd have the kettle full.

The guards pointed out that there were wells all

over town as she ran past their post.

After the fourth trip, her arms ached. The speed of her gait had slowed, too. The laughter from the guards had grown, as did the number of comments.

When she made it up to the kettle, it seemed she would need one more trip. Kal wasn't anywhere to be seen.

The fifth sprint, though, brought her back in time to see Kal standing next to a tub. He was scooping the hot water from the kettle and pouring it in the bath. At least the water was being used for more than her training. "There, I've filled your stupid kettle," she said, as she poured the two buckets in and then flopped down to the ground.

"It doesn't look full to me."

"That's because you've started filling the bath, which you sorely need, by the way."

Kal was silent. He just stood there looking at the three quarters filled kettle.

For an hour she trudged back and forth. On her last trip up to the kettle, she found Kal in the tub, and a woman from the inn was scratching his back.

Callista wasn't going to let him think he'd gotten under her skin, though he already had. "Anything else, my lord?"

"Get yourself something to eat, and when you're done breaking the fast, we'll get on the road. Marl is inside," Kal said, his eyes closed as the giggling woman scrubbed him well under the waterline.

Only a few people were eating when she walked in room. Marl was at a table near the bar, and the smell of eggs, bacon, and bread filled the air. She sat down, and a pleasantly plump woman brought her a plate with a smile.

With a knowing look, Marl asked, "Did you enjoy sleeping in?"

Callista ignored him and dug into the food. It was a simple meal, much like the ones she always had back home, but something about today's eggs and bacon tasted terrific. When she sopped up the last bit of runny yolk with the bread, the attentive woman asked if she'd like another plate, to which she said, "Yes, please."

When she'd wiped that plate clean, Marl stood up and said, "Shall we get on the road?"

Getting up was more of a challenge than she expected. Her legs had grown stiff, and the muscles were beginning to ache. She remembered the first time her gran had her chop wood. The pain after was memorable. The fact that it got worse the next day made her cringe a little to think what tomorrow would bring. She followed Marl outside.

Kal had the horses ready. All their gear was already in the saddlebags. She noticed that both men had a wry look on their faces, but she wasn't sure why.

Marl swung himself into the saddle.

Kal held the reins of Callista's horse as she lifted her leg to the stirrup. The first attempt left her a little short as the pain shot up her leg. She didn't look at Kal, but tried again and forced her foot in, took a breath to brace against the pain she was sure was coming, and hoisted herself onto her mount. It was worse than she imagined, but she hadn't cried out.

Kal hopped up onto his mare like a man who didn't have a care in the world. "I'll ride up front; Callista needs a bath."

She didn't find that comment funny.

Marl and Kal couldn't control their laughter.

They rode easily for the first hour of the morning and then Kal pulled his bow off his shoulders and handed it to his protégé. "It's time to begin today's training."

"What?"

The horses followed the road. Callista could set the reins down and draw the bow without worry. And that's what he wanted her to do. Sets of ten pulls, as far as she could, and then to switch arms.

The first couple of sets were fine, but she could tell her chest and arms were going to burn. By the fifth set, tiny beads of sweat were glistening on her brow. The cold morning air helped, but it wasn't enough.

When they stopped for lunch, she could barely lift her arms. She almost fell trying to get off the horse.

They let the horses graze while they sat on the side of the road, drank from their water skins, and ate jerky. It was a beautiful day, and there hadn't been many people on the way.

When it was time to ride, Marl suggested that their young archery student might have had enough for day one. Kal agreed, albeit a bit reluctantly.

Miserable as she felt, the pain wasn't enough to dampen her enthusiasm for being "on the road." Since she was little, she'd wanted to be an adventurer. Now, here she was seeing the world outside of her gran's cottage and the capital city streets. Admittedly, they were heading back to the capital, now, which seemed like retracing their steps and losing valuable time, but it was still a road she'd never traveled. She thought about her mum.

When she was ten, her mother rode out from the cottage on an adventure. Callista had spent hours each day watching the gap in the trees where the road disappeared into the forest, waiting for her to return. That had been nine years ago. The quest was supposed to have taken a week. There was some part of her that looked for her mum in the face of each stranger they passed.

The beauty of the land was immense. Every flower, tree, and farmhand working a field, filled her with wonder. It was all so new, and this was just the beginning. Who knew what things she would see on their adventure?

They made it to Mossbrook, a tiny little hamlet not far from Marl's Inn. It was easier to get a room there than ride the extra ten kilometers out of their way to stay at Marl's place. He had said he was tired of losing time, so they got a room, ate some dinner, and then went right to bed.

The next morning came just as Callista had feared, with Kal poking her with an arrow. She rolled over, and the stiffness made her moan a little. "I'll be down in a minute so you can continue to torture me." This seemed to satisfy Kal, and he left. Everything ached, but she found she didn't mind it so much and, in a strange way, was curious to see what he had planned. There wasn't a stream nearby, as far as she could tell.

Outside, near a small stand of trees, Kal stood twisting and stretching. It was another beautiful morning, and each breath seemed filled with possibility.

"I don't see any buckets," she said.

"Here, grab this branch."

She did as she was told.

"Now, pull it down to the ground near your left foot."

Callista pulled, and the sapling bent but didn't break. The closer she got to the branch to ground the harder it was to pull, but she made it. "Now, do sets of ten and change arms. Go until I tell you to stop."

For the next hour, she pulled. Her lower back strained under the constant up and down. When the food was ready, Kal said she'd done enough.

The day's ride from Cander to Mossbrook had been a long one. They'd had to walk, trot, and gallop the horses most of the afternoon to maximize their distance. Today's ride would be slightly shorter, and they should reach her gran's place around sunset.

Callista listened to Marl and Kal talk as they rode. She wanted to learn everything about them, and they mostly seemed to want to tell stories of the good old days.

Marl was eager to find out if Elora had done as he had guessed and headed to Trentfri. He regretted not staying together. This backtracking had cost them a week, and who knew how many more days they would need to find her.

When they finally reached her gran's cottage, it had taken them only five days, not seven like Marl had initially estimated. Making up all that time had been hard on the horses, but now they could get some rest.

The silver witch didn't seem at all surprised to see them ride up.

Marl asked, "How did you know we'd be back so soon?"

"I'm wise in many ways. Some leaves tell us much. The scrying pool can show one more than you imagine. The young man who rode out three days ago and told me about the message you sent via the bird, well, he gave me an inkling you'd be back soon. Though, I thought you wrote it would take a few more days."

That night was filled with stories of Callista's first adventure. And Jenson, who was still weak, but improving, joined them, too.

CHAPTER SEVENTEEN

All day she had looked for a sign. Her sisters were less bartenders and more birthday girls all day. The bar receipts showed it, as they didn't bother charging most of the regulars. It was this way every year on their birthday. It was so well known that the sisters were buying, that the day had almost become a holiday.

Trilina liked order. She was meticulous about the books, but her sisters worked hard and took a few days off. They could afford it. She even had a couple of drinks, too, which rarely happened.

Now, on day two of their twenty-eighth year, her mind was on her mother's words. If the sign didn't come until the end of the year, she was going to drive herself nuts. With so few coins to count, the books were done more quickly than usual. She did what she always did when there were spare moments, and she turned to her spell list.

Her mother had laid out precisely the order she was to learn each spell and how to practice. Perfecting the spells wasn't easy. Learning to cast a ghost missile, which would fill the person struck with the sense that an undead soldier was attacking them, was one thing. Figuring out how to cast it in secret and know it worked was another.

A few hours per day she would go on a walk through the Dark Alley neighborhood. In the Dark Alley, there were plenty of thieves and scoundrels around every corner. They didn't mess with her because everyone loved the sisters, but she found these degenerates made great test subjects.

She got the idea one day when she noticed a habitual drug user slicing the coin purse off a local woman who should have known better than leave it exposed. Still, it wasn't right. The code was to never steal from those who lived in Dark Alley. He broke it, and that made Trilina mad.

She cast the spell with the slightest of hand gestures in the thief's direction. One might expect that there would be some flash or a streak of light, but this spell didn't have any of that. Just an invisible projectile that if aimed properly, would hit the target and cause the illusion.

She knew it had worked because the thief screamed, dropped the purse, and ran. That was almost eleven months ago. The man she'd hit with the spell had gotten off the drugs, and for the first time in twenty years, found a job. He had a position cleaning out stables. She had scared him straight.

When it was time to learn her first summoning spell, she picked from a list and decided a wolf might be handy. It was a complicated spell, and she studied the wording for over a week. When she was sure she had it down, Trilina went into the forest and cast the spell.

The creature would come into being and be there to fight for a full minute before being sent back to whatever plane of existence it belonged. The problem is that summoning a creature that is supposed to battle by your side, when you're not in a fight, leaves the animal confused. It had been there less than ten seconds when a traveling merchant just happened to be coming down the road.

The wolf charged.

She had to think fast.

The merchant froze. His horses panicked.

Just before the leaping beast sunk its teeth into the poor man's animals, she unleashed a stun spell. The wolf dropped, and then she hit it again with the same spell, to be sure.

The original summoning spell died, and the wolf disappeared.

She felt so sorry that she bought everything the poor merchant had for sale. He never really understood what had happened; all he knew was she had saved him. When he came back through six months later, he had collected several bottles of liquor that were incredibly rare and refused to take a single copper for them.

Keeping her training secret was a challenge. The

challenge was, she didn't have anyone to ask for help. The descriptions in the book were good, but sometimes the nuance required just wasn't explained well enough.

Regardless, she kept at it.

CHAPTER EIGHTEEN

The next morning Callista heard Kal's footsteps and, without opening her eyes, pointed a finger and said, "I'm getting up. Keep your arrow to yourself."

Kal was waiting with his feet propped up on a log, leaning back in his chair. "Do you know where the messenger post is in town?"

"Of course."

"Can you remember a message if I give it to you without writing it down?"

"Yes."

"Do you know how to write?"

"Yes, Gran taught me," she said, slightly offended.

"It's not a strange question. If I'm honest, I didn't learn to read or write until I was twenty-five. I didn't see the point, but this isn't about me. I need you to take a message and send a bird to Dorodia. Mark it for Elora and write, 'Waiting for you in Trentfri, signed

Kal and Marl.' Or better yet, put your gran's place." He flipped her a silver coin.

"Got it," she said and started to walk toward town.

Kal cleared his throat.

She turned back, and he flicked his knife into the ground. "Be quick about it. The sun is moving."

Her legs still had some lingering pain. It wasn't going to stop her. The messenger post was a two-story building next to the market. Through the gate, she sprinted. All the guards in town knew Callista. The younger ones had been trying to catch her eye for years. The silver witch did not let her granddaughter date. Still, they always waved and smiled when she passed.

The clerk at the messenger office, a bespectacled older black man with worn skin, a sunny disposition, and a bald head greeted her. Callista had been coming to his office since she was little. "Good morning, how are you today?'

"I'm great, Carl, but in a hurry, sorry. I've been on an adventure, we fought spiders, found some treasure, and I'm learning to be a master archer. I'll tell you the story when I have time. Right now, I need to get this message on a bird." She dropped the silver coin down and grabbed a tiny piece of paper on the counter. She scrawled the message with her best penmanship, rolled it up, and handed it to Carl.

She turned to leave.

"Hold on, Callista; you didn't tell me where I'm sending the bird?"

"Sorry, Dorodia. Talk to you later, Carl," she said

with a wave and ran out.

When she got back to Kal, her gran and Marl were up, too. She slid to a stop next to the knife. The shadow had crossed the line.

Kal shook his head. "Well, that won't do at all, will it?"

"It's just barely past."

"Are you familiar with the ancient training method called the push-up?"

"Yes, but come on…"

"I think a fair penalty would be fifty of them."

Callista looked at Raina, who was stirring a pot of something on the fire.

Her grandmother shrugged. "I'd have made you do a hundred, but I'm not a softie like Kal."

She got on the ground and started. When she finished, Kal said, "Okay, do you know where the messenger post is?"

Her eyes flashed. "You know I do."

"Good, I was worried you'd gotten lost last time. Hustle back there and send the same message to Wexstone." Kal threw her another coin.

"Why didn't you have me…" she stopped mid-sentence knowing the futility of arguing. It was about the training. She sighed, pulled the knife from the ground, drew a line, and handed it to Kal. She set her feet and said, "I'm ready."

He flicked the knife, and she was off.

CHAPTER NINETEEN

Heads turned to stare as Matilda was escorted down a gap between the tents. She tried not to panic, fear making her heart flutter like little wings attempting to burst from her chest. It wasn't comfortable. She didn't like it.

Of course, she didn't like anything else about the current situation either. Being marched under sword point into a camp full of soldiers who worship a dragon you have only heard of in horror stories wasn't anyone's idea of fun.

To make it worse, she suspected the person she'd trusted, Elora, had led her there to get caught. That was the way it appeared. Elora had disappeared right when Matilda had needed her most. It didn't make Matilda think happy thoughts.

Although there was one possible bonus, these people had probably taken her parents too.

But as she hurried past more and more of the tents, she noticed they were full of soldiers. No one here was a prisoner, except for her.

A large, deep-red dome filled the middle of the camp, its opening held up by thick metal poles. Guards stood statue-still on either side.

This tent must be the commander's base. Here is where my fate will be decided, she thought

Matilda tried to look brave, sticking her chin in the air and striding along as she imagined her father might. She doubted it fooled anyone. Both her hands shook, and she still bit down on her lip, but it was the best attempt she could make.

The guards stared at her as she marched closer, but neither spoke or moved as she was escorted inside.

It took a moment for her eyes to adjust to the dim lighting. Blinking to help, she looked around her.

In the middle was a large table. A map with wooden figures laid out on it adorned the surface. Random objects weighted each corner. One a metal gauntlet an armored knight might wear, another an ornate drinking goblet. Some of the jewels were missing, but the gold settings still flickered with the reflected light of a massive fire.

Above the fire was a set of metal plates and tubes that funneled the smoke out of a hole in the tent. And standing near it, eating some stew out of a wooden bowl was a man wearing the rest of the knight's armor.

The single bare hand clutched a wooden spoon, moving back and forth between the container and his mouth.

One of her escorts coughed to get his attention. He didn't react until he'd scraped the last morsel out.

Immediately he looked at her, his eyes fixing on her face as if he'd known she was there all along.

Matilda's resolve faltered under his stare, but she did her best to hold his gaze.

"Report," He said, barking the word at the soldiers despite not looking away. With the silence broken, the tension eased.

"We found this girl sneaking along the east side of the camp. Spying on us," the soldier's voice wavered just a little, but enough for Matilda to pick up on it. It helped her relax.

"So, you came to see Aldrei's army, did you?"

"No. I came to find my parents."

"Alone?"

"Yes. You took my parents."

"I've helped a lot of people see sense these past few months."

"They already had enough sense," Matilda replied. They were the most sensible people she knew. That's why they'd decided to travel with the merchants. It came with plenty of guards.

"She was calling for someone called Elora," the soldier said, betraying her. If Matilda hadn't been in the presence of others, she might have sworn.

"Elora… hmmm."

"Elora's my pony," she blurted out, not sure she sounded very convincing.

"Your pony?"

"Yes." Think, Matilda, think. *If you're going to lie you need to be believable.*

"That's not a very normal sort of name for a pony," the Knight replied. She couldn't blame him for being skeptical. It sounded ridiculous to her too.

"I'm not a normal sort of person. I also play the lute..." Matilda reached for the instrument she had slung over her back, grasping the neck.

The Knight held up his hand, cutting off her words and motions. The strings made a twang as she let go, the only sound in the moment that followed. It took some self-control not to laugh. She fought it down to a small smirk, but the Knight didn't look as amused.

"Take her to our lady. See she's allocated to a section and taken under the wing of a devout. She can be instructed as her parents must have been."

"Instructed?" she asked as the soldier grabbed her arm to pull her away.

The Knight locked eyes with her again.

"Yes. You will learn our ways. All do and come to accept Aldrei as their God."

He waved his hand towards the entrance and turned his back on them.

Matilda didn't like the sound of this. It made her think of school. Or something worse.

"This way," said the soldier with his sword still pointed at her. She didn't hesitate as he motioned for her to lead the way. You didn't argue with people wielding sharp objects in your direction. That much Matilda already knew.

The route took her to the opposite side of the camp, off in the distance she could see the Fog that lingered like an ever-present threat. It rose so high, she wasn't sure how close it was, but still, Matilda shivered. How could they all live so close to it?

On this side of the camp the tents were more rigidly laid out, and larger, flaps open at each entrance just wide enough for her to see rows and rows of beds inside each one. They were all empty, the beds neatly covered in green blankets. The kind that looked like they itched.

"New recruit?" a young man said from outside the next tent.

"Yup," the sword-wielding soldier replied. "Caught a stray from one of the earlier groups. She's here for processing."

"Best get her to The Lady then. She likes to see them all before they start."

Matilda raised her eyebrows at this strange conversation. Who was The Lady? And why didn't she have a name?

She didn't have to wait long for answers. The younger sentry pushed the flap of the tent behind him out of the way. Nudged towards the entrance, Matilda had little choice but to go inside.

Once more she tried to raise her chin and appear unafraid. This time it was a little easier.

Hundreds of candles cast a warm light about The Lady's tent. Everywhere she looked were little tables, flat-topped chests, and luggage crates. All around were wax sentinels, each bearing a tiny flickering flame.

It took Matilda a moment to notice there was a single exception, near the back of the tent. A low table, only inches from the floor, in front of a cross-legged woman, caught her eye. Swirling in the middle of a globe in front of the woman was a white fog, just like the cloud that hung to the north-west of the camp.

The woman stared at it, her lips moving in a silent chant.

Matilda watched, mesmerized until a noise from behind made her turn.

Both soldiers were gone, the flap shut behind them. She was alone with The Lady.

"Come, Matilda Liron," the woman said. "Sit with me and talk."

***

Rhysdan blinked as he stood, trying not to move. Behind him was a raw recruit tent. Empty except for a single person. A woman, barely older than a girl.

It was his assignment to keep an eye on her until morning. Just like everyone who emerged from The Lady's tent, she had come out with her eyes glazed over, silent and malleable. They'd encouraged her to bed and would wait to see if she turned out like the majority, eager to serve Andrei, or if she would reject whatever fancy trick was meant to have happened.

Unlike most of the camp, Rhysdan had never been inside The Lady's tent. And he had no desire to. So far, no one seemed to have noticed that he'd been missed out.

When he'd arrived in camp, he'd been alone, found after a fishing trip on the nearby lake. They'd added him to a large group of people, and he'd paid attention.

Every afternoon and evening the people were taken off to see Her. They were gone for an hour, and they came back like walking ghosts.

There was no set pattern to how many were dealt with like this each day.

One day he noted she had stopped earlier than usual, so he had snuck out the tent and hid. An hour later he'd adopted the trance-like state and wandered aimlessly.

It hadn't taken long for Rhysdan to be spotted. The washerwoman who'd found him had escorted him to the nearby tent and told him to rest.

Every day since he'd pretended to think Aldrei was the greatest being in existence.

Rhysdan yawned. It was tiring spending every moment faking enthusiasm. He just wanted to go home.

As he thought of his small cottage nestled at the foot of a hill, he noticed a movement in the shadows. Moving the torch he carried, he tried to shed more light in that direction.

A frown fixed itself on his face when the dancing flames showed him little more than the loose canvas of the tent, flapping in the breeze. The stake had come out of the ground on that section, letting the wind play with the edges like a cat with ribbon.

Not wanting the young woman inside to get too cold, he fixed it back in place.

There, he thought. *I've done a good deed.*

Back in position, Rhysdan tried to put the incident from his mind, but something wasn't right.

For several seconds he stared into space, his gut telling him he had best not relax, but his brain unable to explain why.

I'll check on the girl. Might help.

Stepping into the tent gave him his answer.

Leaned over the bed was a cloaked figure.

"Matilda," the sneak whispered, reaching to shake the girl's shoulder and wake her up.

A friend, then. Someone was trying to rescue her. And not a stake pulled out by the wind after all.

"Don't wake her," he said, keeping his voice as quiet as he could while still making sure she heard.

The figure whirled around to face him, shock registering on her face. Her hood fell as she moved, showing her glossy brown hair.

For what felt like an age they stared at each other —neither moving.

"I need to wake her. We shouldn't be here," the woman said.

"Most people say that at first. But they don't eventually. And she might not either in the morning," Rhysdan motioned to the sleeping form.

"What have you done to her?"

"I've not done anything. The Lady has. No idea what. I managed to avoid it."

"Will she be alright?" The woman glanced at the

girl's sleeping face, a mix of curiosity and concern on her face.

"As long as you don't wake her."

"But..."

"I know, you shouldn't be here. But I won't tell if you don't." Rhysdan smiled.

She raised her eyebrows.

"Get some sleep as well. It will look less suspicious if someone does decide to come and check up on me," Rhysdan said pointing his thumb at his chest.

"I'll need to leave before it's light."

"I know. She'll wake up naturally before then. They often do."

The woman nodded and sat on the bed beside her friend.

"Why are you helping me?" she asked before he could return to his post.

He thought about the question. Why was he helping her? So far he'd not put a foot out of place, but the answer was obvious. This woman was the first person that he'd spoken to in weeks not brainwashed into believing Aldrei was a God. It felt good. Until that moment he hadn't realized how much he'd missed it.

"I'm not one of them," he replied. The woman nodded and unclipped her cloak. For now, at least, she had chosen to trust him.

***

The sound of whispering broke through Matilda's thoughts. Two people. One voice she recognized.

"I thought you said she'd be awake by now," the familiar voice said.

"Some take a little longer. And one or two never woke up at all."

"What do you mean, one or two never woke up?"

"It is what it is. Nothing any of us can do about it."

Matilda frowned as she opened her eyes.

Standing nearby, a hand on her shoulder was a woman wearing a dark green travel cloak. Only a meter behind her was an armed guard. She did her best to recall where she was and who these people were, but nothing came to mind.

"Matilda?" the woman said. "You all right?"

"Uhhhh... I think so."

Yes, there was nothing wrong with her; she thought as she sat up and pushed the blanket back. *But where is the dragon?* She could hear his voice in her head, telling her she was a most devoted servant.

But she'd never met a dragon, had she?

"Come on, Matilda, we've got to get out of here," the woman said.

Matilda opened her mouth to ask them who they were, but the name popped into her head. This was Elora, and Elora had been helping her.

"Right," she replied. "We have to find Marl."

"Who is Marl?" the guard asked.

"My brother-in-law." Elora helped Matilda to her feet.

"Good. If she still remembers people, then there's a good chance The Lady didn't finish her task. It can take several sessions to make it permanent."

"Of course, I can still remember people," Matilda replied, but she sounded far more confident than she was. It had taken her a minute to remember Elora. Now it came flooding back to her—their adventure in the forest, finding the abandoned village and then this army.

The guard doused his torch, plunging them both into almost total darkness.

"Come," he said. I know the quickest way out of camp. At this time of the morning, it should be quiet too."

Matilda didn't argue. Taking her lute off Elora, she slung it over her back.

Weaving past tent after tent, the three of them hurried along. It wouldn't be long until dawn, and then the encampment would come alive.

Despite keeping low when they were out in the open and checking for signs of other people at every tent corner, they were soon at one edge. Their guide had led them true.

A wall of smell hit Matilda, almost knocking her over. She wrinkled up her nose.

"Is that what I think it is?" Elora asked before she could comment.

"An army has to go to the toilet somewhere," he replied. "But what soldier lingers here? The best place to try and sneak out."

He had a point, even if it was a smelly one. Before

sun up this part of the camp was deserted.

Creeping along the edge of the cordoned-off pit latrines, they hurried toward a mountain. Matilda had just passed the final one when she heard a shout from behind her.

Their guard froze.

"Go," he said a moment later, pulling out his sword to defend them. Elora drew her own and planted her feet beside him.

"Not alone," she replied. "You've risked everything to help. Come with us."

All too quickly more soldiers appeared, raised by the cry of their comrade.

At least six men rushed the trio, all of them brandishing swords. Matilda wanted to surrender, raising her arms on instinct. She'd never been in a fight.

But both Elora and their guide sprang into action, meeting steel with steel.

Sparks of scraping metal lit up their determined faces as side by side they drove the first soldiers back.

But one got past, eyes fixed on Matilda, sword darting and slashing. She took several steps backward, her mind blank, her body wanting to run but having nowhere to go.

Something caught her foot, sending her sprawling backward into a muddy puddle. As the soldier lifted his blade to strike, Matilda stretched out her hand and arm in an attempt to protect herself.

A jet of steam shot from her fingertips, hitting the soldier in the chest. He screamed and dropped his sword.

Matilda gaped.

Had she just done that?

There was no time to find out. More soldiers poured out of the tents in the distance.

Elora parried a thrust from the remaining fighter, the rest dead or injured. He didn't stand a chance as she flicked her sword deftly and sliced it downward. It made the deadly strike look effortless and graceful.

"Now it's time to go," she said, grabbing their guide's arm to pull him away.

Matilda scrambled to her feet, noticing the puddle she'd fallen into was gone. Dry, cracked dirt in its place.

Something magical had happened. But what? she thought as she ran beside Elora.

"This way," their guide called, veering off to the left, to one side of a large lake.

They were soon splashing in ankle deep water that stretched for meters. Reeds grew high and swayed in the wind, the rustle as they brushed against each other drowning out the sound of pursuit.

Right before they ran into the large bed of head-high plants, he stretched out his arm and took Elora's hand. She then did the same to Matilda, forming a chain so none of them would lose each other.

Somehow, they kept up the pace, rushing blindly onward into deeper water. Thick reed stalks caught Matilda in the face, stinging the skin until she had the sense to raise her arm like a shield.

By the time they were out the other side, they were

almost waist deep in the lake.

As one, they stopped splashing. The lake sat at the foot of a mountain, with only the camp in-between. It was lit up by the dawning sun, which made it look both magnificent and daunting.

"Follow me as quietly as you can," their guide whispered before continuing left along the edge of the reeds, now moving far slower.

Matilda was grateful for the break, but she didn't linger behind. She couldn't remember what had happened once she'd sat down at the table with The Lady, but she knew one thing for sure. She didn't want to go back.

With each minute that passed with no signs of pursuit, Matilda relaxed.

"We should be safe now," the man said. "The soldiers won't go this far from the camp without explicit orders."

They waded to the shore, no one saying anything else as they sat down on some dry grass.

They'd escaped. Just.

The silence between them was full in its way. Freedom was theirs, and it should have made Matilda elated and grateful, but it was tainted.

Did I do something magical? Matilda asked herself. She didn't know the answer. And a big part of her had no desire to find out.

CHAPTER TWENTY

Marl was anxious. Kal had Callista to train and mess with, and he was enjoying himself. Marl just had thoughts of the time lost running all over the land looking for Kal and now trying to find Elora.

He chopped wood. When there wasn't any more to chop, he cleaned the stables. Next, he repaired a fence behind the cottage.

All the while, Raina watched the fire, hummed a tune, and asked him to join her. When he ran out of things to do, he sat down.

Kal had gone off to find a pint. Callista, worn from her morning of message sending, passed out in her bed.

"What are you brewing?" Marl asked.

"I'm making another batch of the balm Callista used on your burns. It's handy stuff."

"I'm sure we'll need it," he said, looking tired and

worn down.

The silver witch was many things, healer, herbalist, and seer, but most of all, she was a loyal friend to those she called 'friend' and Marl was one of her oldest. She had listened when he went half-mad after losing his family. It was her idea for him to start the inn. When a local tradesman had gotten it in his head that having a witch living near the city walls was a danger to society, it was Marl who had visited him late one night and left him bruised and of a new mind.

It wasn't Marl's way to be an enforcer, but he didn't tolerate anyone messing with his friends.

The day was colder than it had been in a long while. Clouds had rolled in, and there was a whiff of pending rain in the air. Raina tended to her brew and Marl watched the flames.

It was clear from his face he had a lot on his mind. Raina knew that he would tell her his fears when he was ready. It was how they had always been since she was a young woman and he was a little boy running errands for her while she was pregnant with her daughter, Callista's mom. They were more than friends; they were family.

When Marl spoke, his voice was soft. "We've wasted too much time."

"Have you?"

"Losing Jenson set us back. Trying to track down Kal, well that took much longer than I had hoped. Now, I have no idea where Elora has gone. I should have gone to meet her, and we could have chased down Kal together."

"Not every detour takes us off the path."

"You know how I get when you start speaking in riddles."

"This isn't a riddle; it's just a fact that sometimes fate puts us exactly where we need to be when we need to be there." Raina's eyes were soft. A cold wind blew up, and the fire danced. "It will be raining soon."

"Did you know, when Callista and I left, that we'd be back so soon?"

"I know more than most, less than a few, and nothing compared to my lost sister, but yes, I was sure you'd pass this way again, and Callista would be better for it."

Marl considered this and nodded his head. "What do you see on our path?"

"I see a storm."

"I meant…"

"I know, and I was being both literal and figurative. The rain in those clouds will dump a downpour on us just after the balm is done. The greater storm is brewing in the mind of the dragon, and I have no idea what it will bring, but I know it is more than you expect and more than I can know."

"And Elora? How long must we wait for her?"

"She will be along just as soon as you solve your problem."

Marl looked at her and then back at the fire. He wasn't sure what problem she was speaking of, and he wasn't sure he wanted to know. The smell of the balm was nice, and his trepidation faded. "What problem is that?"

"Your party needs a wizard."

"We didn't need one last time," he said, showing his dislike for those who fight with spells. Marl believed it was cheating, though he had to admit he didn't mind having enchanted weapons or armor when it could be had. In his heart, though, he thought battle should be between two souls, a clash of wits and steel.

"This time you do," Raina said, taking the pot off the fire and setting it on the ground next to the door of the cottage. She put the lid on the pot, turned back to Marl and said, "We should go inside."

A bolt of lightning flashed. The clouds opened up, and a wall of rain ran over the forest toward the cottage. Marl stood and walked inside behind her, just as the storm reached the porch. He knew Raina was right, but he didn't have to like it.

CHAPTER TWENTY-ONE

For an hour the rain poured down. When it stopped, the last sunlight of the day glistened off the wet ground in front of the cottage. Marl got some dry wood and started the fire again, while Raina chopped some vegetables for dinner.

Callista came out of the cottage, stretching. "I'm pretty sure Kal is trying to kill me."

Raina shook her head. "I let you get lazy around here. You do what he says."

With a shrug, she said, "I'm going into town. I'll grab something to eat there and let you old people get caught up." And off she trotted with the exuberance and sass of youth.

Marl and Raina looked at each other knowing they had been that young once, but not quite remembering what it was like.

Raina looked down at the veggies she was cutting

and stopped. "You know what I'm thinking?"

"In all the seasons that I've known you, I've never known."

She walked to the pen where she kept two hogs and slid the cut vegetables off the cutting board into their trough.

Marl looked at her and raised a brow.

She answered his look with, "Those gals at the Third Eye serve up some pretty good stew, and their bread is always fresh. Amazing, considering it's in Dark Alley. And I could use a beer. Let me get my walking stick, and then I'm taking you to dinner."

She came back out of the cottage with a lace shawl around her shoulders and a polished stick that looked part cane and part wizard's staff. "Come on; I know a short cut through town that will get us there in no time."

Marl wasn't going to question his old friend, partly because nobody said 'no' to the silver witch and partly out of respect.

She walked faster than he expected. The moment they got through the main gate, she said "Hello" to the commander of the guard, who was sitting on a bench outside his office smoking and then walked right past him, behind his desk, through a door, through another door, and into a narrow walkway.

They followed the city walls for a while, then cut through the back door of a butcher shop, crossed the street and climbed up the stairs of a fine tailor. The owner commented on how well she looked and didn't mind at all when she passed through his shop on the way to stairs that went up to an adjacent building's roof.

This part of town was a side of the capital he had never seen.

Raina took them over three rooftops, including a leap of a meter which she didn't even pause before taking. From there they went back down some stairs into an intimate courtyard that had grown out of buildings sprouting up around it. On the other side, a red door to a brothel, which as far as Marl could tell, didn't have an entrance on Main Street.

All the ladies said "Hi," to Raina as she sauntered past. A few of the men gave her a nod, too. One of them tried to hide, but she wistfully said, "Say 'Hi' to Bella, I'll be sure to mention to her that I ran into you at the market next time I see her."

The man looked relieved.

Raina was known to be able to keep a secret if she liked a person.

They meandered their way through the depths of the Dark Alley until they reached a plain brown door with a triangle on it. This time she knocked three times and then two quick ones.

"Come on in, Aunt Raina," said the voice.

Raina introduced Marl to her niece. She explained that Trilina was the eldest of her late sister's triplets, told the story of the clever wager that her nieces played on unsuspecting guests and bragged up the chili. Then showed Marl through to the bar.

Brilina and Frilina both gave their aunt a big hug.

The crowded bar buzzed as people talked and ate

all around. It was always a festive atmosphere at the Third Eye. Marl saw Kal at the bar and invited him over to eat with them at their table.

Just as they got settled, had their first drinks in hand, and were telling stories, Callista walked in. She saw them and asked, "I came straight here from the cottage. How in the world did you two get here before me?"

Raina held up her hands innocently. "I don't know, dear. Us old people walk so slowly; it's hard to imagine we would travel so far at all, let alone get here before someone as young as you."

Callista didn't fight it. She grabbed a chair and sat down. "One day you'll need to tell me how you did it?"

"Can't an old woman have a few secrets?"

Everyone laughed.

The evening was full of laughter, food, and drink. Tales from the old days flowed as smoothly as the wine.

As it got late into the evening, and the crowd thinned, talk turned to more pressing matters. Marl was still anxious about finding Elora, but Raina assured him that their paths would cross sooner than he could imagine. She always did that, talked in mystical hints, and it made Marl shake his head.

"Can't you just share what you know?"

"The tea leaves are not specific," Raina said.

Callista laughed. "When did you ever read tea leaves?"

"Hush, girl. It's a saying."

Fantasy Series

Kal said, "The tea leaves are not specific? That's a saying? How come I've never heard it."

Marl shook his head in agreement. "Nope, that's not a saying at all. Give it up, have you scried out fate?"

By this time, all three sisters had come over, the bar left tended by a jolly older bald man, and pulled up chairs. "Yes, Auntie, do tell us what the future brings," said Brilina as she hugged her aunt and sat down next to her.

Raina said, "There is another old saying, 'Don't tease an old witch or you'll wake up a forest toad.'"

Marl raised his glass and said, "Now, that is a saying I believe. To old witches and their wise counsel."

Everyone raised their drinks.

The evening wore on.

Eventually, the bar closed, but the seven remained. Marl learned all about the sisters, the tragic loss of their parents, and how they had become respected business tycoons with Trilina at the helm.

She blushed at the compliment but accepted it with grace. "Thank you, but we all worked equally hard."

Her sisters would have none of it. They both went back and forth telling stories about how Trilina seemed never to sleep, worked constantly, and had the best business mind in the land. When Brilina finished her last story of her sister, she gave a bit of a sigh. "She's going to leave us this year, though."

Frilina gasped. "Is that what Mom told you in the

letter, the post-script?"

"Yes. I wasn't supposed to tell you what was in it, but Mom said that this year Trilina would have to leave the business after our twenty-eighth birthday, which struck me as odd at the time. Why not write the farm, but I guess she knew?"

"That's what she wrote in mine, too!"

The table had gotten silent.

Everyone looked at the two sisters, who then turned to their sister and said at the same time, "Why do you have to leave?"

A long silence followed. Frilina and Brilina looked like their hearts were breaking.

******

Trilina sat with her sisters and the friends her aunt had brought to the bar and couldn't move. She had been waiting for two days for a sign. Had this been it?

She opened her mouth to answer Frilina's and Brilina's question but couldn't find the words. A long deep breath and she tried again—still, nothing.

Nobody around the table moved.

Trilina brought her glass to her mouth. She set it back down again without taking a sip. "I honestly don't know. Mom told me that this was the year something happened, that I would get a sign, and it would mean leaving here for a while," she said and then turned to her aunt. "Do you know what the sign was supposed to be?"

The aunt looked at Marl, who was leaning back

and basking in the comfort of the many drinks he'd had through and since dinner.

"Don't look at me. I'm trying to figure out how to find a mage willing to run off and chase that stupid dragon. Are you a powerful wizard, Trilina?"

Her sisters laughed.

Brilina gave Trilina a loving punch in the arm. "This one can't even cook a proper stew. She's all numbers and ledgers, spends her whole life figuring out how to keep us up to our ears in gold coins."

Frilina was rolling. "If ledgers were magic, then she's your girl."

Trilina sat like a statue. She didn't respond to her sisters' good-natured ribbing. She just looked at Marl expressionless. If she was looking for a sign, well, this one was flashing brighter than the morning star.

The knowing look on Raina's face didn't go unnoticed. Marl saw it, then Brilina and Frilina. Raina asked, "Have you been studying, dear?"

She looked at her sisters, then back at Marl, and finally to her aunt. "I've been doing what Mom asked."

The bartender, with two of the kitchen staff by his side, said from the front door, "We're heading out, boss."

Trilina thanked them and said, "I'll lock up. Great work tonight."

And they were alone.

Nobody said a word. The drinks sat on the table. The question hung in the air. It would not be ignored.

It was Brilina who broke the silence. "Have you

been studying magic? Is that what's in those books you're always reading?"

With a soft, quiet voice that was more fourteen-year-old frightened girl than twenty-eight-year-old head of the family, she said, "Yes."

The silence that followed was heavy. It seemed everyone had questions, and none of them could be asked.

Raina pulled a pipe out and used the candle to light it. She puffed a few rings of smoke and then drew in a deep breath. From her mouth unfurled a smoke dragon.

The silence was deafening, almost painful, until Kal said, "Well, as far as signs go, that's the best I've ever seen. Welcome to the team, lassie."

And like a fading morning mist, the tension was gone, the sisters hugged, and Raina nodded with the deep satisfaction of an old woman who knows a secret or two.

CHAPTER TWENTY-TWO

Matilda's feet hurt. They'd been walking along the edge of the lake most of the morning. At first, she'd appreciated the space to think.

Her memories of the previous day were still hazy. She knew she'd talked to The Lady for a while and sat at the table, but she couldn't remember any more than that. And she didn't recall how Aldrei the dragon played a part. Somehow, she knew the sound of his voice. Of everything that she remembered that was one detail that remained.

Aldrei's voice.

To make her even more anxious, she also couldn't be sure if she had or hadn't done something magical. A soldier had attacked her until steam had jetted from her hand somehow absorbing the puddle.

Everyone knew magic existed, but like the Fog, it was the stuff of stories. People didn't perform magic.

Anything magical was reserved for the five, far away in their tower. Or rumors of healers, witches, and the occasional mediocre wizard who might or might not turn you into a toad for being naughty.

It wasn't the kind of thing an average girl from an ordinary village did in the heat of battle. Especially not by accident.

On top of all that, Matilda missed her parents. When captured, she'd hoped to find them, but somehow, she knew they weren't in the camp anymore. Something The Lady had said lingered on the edge of her memory. She remembered asking where they were, but the reply stayed just out of reach, the answer lost, in a fog of its own.

Letting out a sigh, Matilda continued to trudge. She didn't have any answers, and she didn't dare voice her questions.

"Let's take a break," Rhysdan said only a second later. As he slowed, he gave her a wink. "My feet are killing me, and I don't know about you two, but I'm starving. We never did manage to get breakfast before we were running for our lives."

"If I hadn't lost my horse, we'd be able to eat and take turns riding," Elora said.

Rhysdan opened his mouth as if to reply before closing it again. Given Elora's mood, Matilda didn't blame him.

Despite her complaint, Elora stopped, and the three of them flopped down on the grass by the lake once more.

The glint of the sun off the ripples on the lake lit

up the side of the mountain behind it. Snow capped the top, the first indication that the cold season was on its way.

"Now we're out of harm's way, where were you ladies thinking of heading? You said something about a guy called Marl?"

Elora nodded. "My brother-in-law. He helped fight off Aldrei last time the dragon was here."

"Then he sounds like my kind of man. If you'll have my company and my sword, I'll see you safe until you meet up with him."

"I assure you, I don't need protecting like some wall-flower," Elora replied. Matilda raised her eyebrows expecting Rhysdan to be offended by the cold response, but he let out a loud chuckle.

"Good. All the better. But I won't sleep well at night, if I walk off and leave you both. And besides, if you're finding him so you can try to stop Aldrei a second time, I can be of assistance. Never much liked the idea of people being brainwashed into worshipping a serpent."

This seemed to ease the tension, and Elora looked thoughtful for a moment. "All right. I want to get to the capital as fast as I can, but we'll need horses."

"Can't our magic wielder here come up with something?" Rhysdan motioned to Matilda, his tone neutral as if he'd asked what she wanted to eat for dinner or what she thought of the weather.

Matilda's cheeks flushed as Elora stared at her. Until that moment she'd never known what it was like to want to be swallowed up whole by a dragon. Now she considered it.

"You can do magic?" Elora asked. "Why didn't you say so?"

"I…" Matilda's words didn't come out as her brain drew a blank.

How could she explain that she hadn't known? That she didn't even know now.

"I don't think I can." She shrugged her shoulders, knowing it wasn't what she wanted to say but unable to find the right words.

"You gave one of those soldiers a good blasting back there," Rhysdan said. "Turned water into steam. Pretty impressive if you ask me."

"I don't know how I did it. I've never done it before." She gulped, wondering what they'd think of her. People were scared of magic users, weren't they? People didn't like to travel with them. They attracted trouble.

"Hmmm…" Elora's eyes lit up. "I think I know just the person who can help us with that. There's a woman we can see on the way to the capitol. She's a healer and a magic user. She'll know how to help you with the gift."

"Gift? You think it's a gift?"

"Of course, my dear. I'm surprised there's no one else in your family who might have thought to look out for it in you."

"My family are all normal."

"Well, the silver witch will know what to do." With these words, Elora stood. "And we'd best be on our way."

"There's a village not far from here. I can get us some horses." Rhysdan gave them both a beaming smile, setting off again to lead the way.

Matilda sighed as she pushed herself up onto her aching feet. She missed her pony. Hopefully one day she'd see it again.

***

What a situation you've got yourself into now, Rhysdan thought to himself as he handed over the map he'd hastily drawn to his cottage.

"I'm only accepting your word I'll find payment here because old Roger says you're good for it. If I find out you've sold me short, I'll make sure your face goes up on posters on every tree between the Fog and sea."

"You'll find more than enough," Rhysdan said, fighting to keep polite. "It's me who has to hope we're not being sold short. Or that you won't rob me blind before I'm back. These horses had better be worth the price."

Rhysdan took the offered reins, leading all three mounts out of the stable. They'd cost him the majority of his savings. Perhaps all of it, depending on how honest the blacksmith was, but he had to be thankful. If the traveling merchant, Roger, hadn't been in the village, they'd not have been taken seriously.

When she saw the horses, Elora's face lit up. He grinned as he handed her the reins to the bigger of the two mares. Before he could ask where Matilda was, he heard the sound of someone playing the lute and singing an old children's song.

"We needed some money for food," Elora explained, beckoning for him to follow.

They walked past the rest of the small businesses in the village until they reached the green outside the inn. Matilda sat on a log, her instrument in her lap, playing and singing while a gaggle of small children sat and clapped at her feet, mesmerized. In between, them, laid out like a nest, was Matilda's cloak.

As they came closer, he spotted several small coins dotting the fabric.

It looks like we'll have some money to keep our bellies full after all.

Rhysdan couldn't help but feel proud of the young lass. She played well too.

Within the hour Matilda had earned them enough coins to buy a blanket apiece, one of the mothers had offered the trio dinner, and several others had put together ration packs for them. They were all set to leave for the capital.

Not bad for a bit of singing and playing, he thought splitting it among the saddlebags they had.

"Thank you," Elora said, barely above a whisper while Matilda fed her new horse an apple. "You didn't have to do this for us. I'll find a way to pay you back."

Rhysdan gave her a nod, not sure how to respond. Until now he'd got the impression, she didn't like him much, or men in general. It was the warmest thing she'd said since they'd met.

Less than ten minutes later they were riding out of the village, several of the children running along, failing to keep up but waving goodbye to Matilda as they did.

As she promised to come back and play for them again someday, he noticed the first genuine smile on her face.

Kids. Something about them that warms the heart.
***

Hanging at the back of the trio, Rhysdan kept an eye out for possible threats. They'd been on the road for just over a day, camping out the previous night under the stars. The blankets and a small fire had kept them warm enough to sleep a few hours, but he had woken up grateful it wasn't yet winter.

"I'm pretty sure there's a town up ahead," Elora said, breaking the silence that sat between them more often than not.

"Do you think there will be an inn?" Matilda replied.

Rhysdan grinned. He'd been thinking the same thing. His bones ached, and his legs were sore. It had been a long time since he'd traveled so far, and he wasn't as young or fit as his companions. A soft bed was a happy thought.

"We've not got enough money to stay at an inn." Elora frowned

"I could offer to play again." Matilda tapped the lute strapped to her back, somehow making a delicate chord ring out. No one needed any convincing. As one they spurred their horses on, pushing them to reach the safety and warmth of civilization before night fell.

Luck be with us, Rhysdan thought, but an hour later they were still riding along the same track, no houses in sight.

Their mounts were slowing, their feet not lifting as high with each step, kicking up more dirt and making it clear, if not for their sake but the horses', they'd need to stop soon.

"Come on, let us find somewhere to rest. This old man wants to put his head on a pillow instead of a tree root tonight."

He concentrated on the road ahead, trying not to shiver as a blast of wind came rushing down the small hill they climbed.

As they neared the top, patters of rain started to fall. Before Rhysdan could suggest they try to find shelter, they crested the hill. Nestled in the valley on the other side was a town.

Matilda let out a cheer as they urged their tired mounts down the last mile.

Most of the town buildings were made of wood, but a few in the center boasted stone walls. Thatching topped each one, and candles and oil lamps lit the windows of a large inn.

The rain had soaked every last inch of their clothing by the time they pulled up outside the stables. The evening had drawn in sooner than usual, the cloud obscuring any sunset.

A stable lad rushed out, eager to assist despite the weather. Wordlessly the boy took the reins and led their horses inside to find food and rest of their own. The trio hurried to the warm light on the other side of the solid oak front door.

It sat ajar and gave way to a gentle touch despite

its weight.

At last, Rhysdan thought as he stepped out of the pouring rain and pulled the hood from his head.

The large room was full of tables, travelers, flickering light and the occasional farm dog. Despite the myriad of conversations in full flow, the entrance of three more people drew glances and a lull in the noise.

Rhysdan hung back, letting the focus shift to the women. Unlike him they wouldn't be seen as a threat and, with Matilda's lute still on her back, they'd hopefully appear to be traveling entertainers.

Given her personality, he expected Matilda to let Elora approach the bar and inquire about playing for their keep, but Matilda strode up to the woman there.

"Good evening, ma'am," Matilda said, getting the attention of the barkeep. "My fellow travelers and I find ourselves short on funds to purchase a pillow for our heads tonight. I'm never without a good instrument and songs to warm a cold night with, however."

The woman smiled down at Matilda, looking over her lute as she pulled it off her back.

"Daryl. It looks like we've got ourselves some entertainment this evening. Lass here reckons she can play."

"Well, get her a stool then, and let's hear if she's any good," a male voice called from an open doorway behind.

Rhysdan fought to hide his grin at their words. They doubted she was going to be able to entertain them, but he already knew she could play.

If Matilda was offended by the doubt they displayed, she didn't show it. Instead, she stepped up to the area that cleared around a three-legged stool. It wobbled as she sat on it, but again she pretended not to notice, her eyes focused on her instrument.

Chairs scraped around to face her, and voices yelled out to let others know something was happening as the patrons all gave her their attention.

"Up past your curfew aren't you, young'un?" someone called. Many laughed, but Matilda didn't so much as blush.

The calm that settled over her as her fingers found the strings and tried a chord was uncanny. It radiated out, silencing the jeers, jokes and laughter bit by bit.

Only when you could hear a pin drop did she play another note, and then another, everyone watching, enchanted.

She didn't sing this time, letting the music do her work for her. A haunting tune that made Rhysdan think of being lost at sea. Shipwrecked. Unable to say goodbye to a loved one.

As he glanced around the room, he doubted he was the only one having such thoughts. Before Matilda finished playing, he saw several patrons, male and female alike, wiping tears from their eyes.

When she struck the last note, Matilda looked up, observing the silent faces for just a fraction.

The spell broke, and in its way Rhysdan didn't doubt it had been a spell.

This woman could do magic. Powerful magic. Bet

her Pa or Ma could too.

Chattering filled the room.

"Another, lass. Play us another."

"Certainly, sir," she replied, grinning. It was a smug grin, and Rhysdan found himself chuckling. She knew she had them captivated for as long as she wanted to play.

When Matilda struck up a jig next, chairs and tables were pushed back, and the younger folk joined each other to dance. This time she sang a familiar folk song, encouraging everyone to join in with her.

Just as Rhysdan thought a drink would wet the whistle enough to join in the Innkeeper came over carrying a tray. It was laden with food and drink for three.

"Your lass can stick around as many nights as she likes. I'll see you all fed and watered for it," the man said.

"Mighty kind of you," Rhysdan replied, taking a full tankard. "But we'll just be here the one."

Elora sat beside him, nodding at Matilda as her hands flew across the lute, setting the pace of the dance.

"Do you think anyone else realizes how much she's bewitching them?" Elora asked, quiet enough only he'd hear her.

"No," Rhysdan replied. "Most common folk don't like being magicked. But I don't think she knows she's doing it either."

"No. She doesn't. We'll need to protect her."

"From them or herself?"

"Possibly, both." Elora's eyes met his, and he nodded back.

They had an understanding. The three of them were a team now, with two swords and a mage.

CHAPTER TWENTY-THREE

If they pushed the horses and changed mounts at Peja, Callista and Trilina could reach her farm in two days. Raina had suggested it was a good idea for Callista to join her cousin, so they could get to know each other, and she could bring Trilina up to speed on what they knew of the dragon.

These would be long days; from Trentfri to Peja was just under one hundred kilometers and then from there to the farm outside of Erylcis was another one hundred and five. Fortunately, she knew Trilina had deep pockets and broader influence.

Callista adored her cousins. When they opened the bar, she worked for a while doing dishes. She'd never had any siblings, and before they had decided to open the Third Eye, she'd only heard stories about them from her gran. As far as role models go, Trilina was a good one.

It was Trilina who taught her math. Brilina showed Callista how to cook dishes that made men's mouth water, and Frilina explained why that was important and how to flirt.

As she rode to the gate, the sun's light hinting that it would be there shortly, she thought about Trilina's secret. How had she kept it from her sisters all these years? Callista knew her fair share of magic, but it was mostly related to the art of healing. She had been taught by the most famous witch in the land. It seemed unimaginable that her cousin had learned it all on her own.

There had always been lots of questions when she got to hang out with Trilina, but they had been more about how she kept her hair so shiny, did she have any boys she liked, how does one know if a boy likes them, and on and on and on. As she thought back about all the time she followed the sisters around like a puppy, Callista got a knot in her gut at how much of a little pest she must have been, but they never seemed to mind.

Still, she thought, she was nineteen now, and her childhood was over. It was time to be a grown-up. The knot went away. It was the first time she'd thought of herself as an adult. Not after the battle with the spiders or the rough days of training, she'd survived, but now, riding toward the gate.

The muscles in her shoulder, which had burned for days after the whole water bucket brigade training, seemed strong. Her legs still ached. They hadn't been given any time to recover. The next four days in the saddle would push her body further. She didn't mind. It was the best kind of pain. Pain with a purpose.

She thought about Kal. He was annoying and smart. Callista wondered if her father had been like him. Her mother had never spoken of the man she hadn't met or called "Dad," only to say he had left them to chase glory. It was the tone of her mother's voice that had carried an edge of disgust with it, which told the tale of how she felt about him. And that her mother would leave for the same reason, well, that thought had been simmering below the surface for years. She had not forgiven her mother and had yearned to meet her father.

As she approached the gate, she reminded herself that Trilina had lost her parents, and she should be thankful that hers might still be out there.

Trilina sat tall in the saddle, back straight, her long dark hair poured over her shoulders like shimmering silk. Dressed in leather riding chaps, a white blouse, and thick brown boots, she looked like she could rule the world. Callista reminded herself that she was past the years of idolizing her cousin.

The broad smile from Trilina made her day.

Trilina said, "Good timing, I just got here. Did you get any sleep?"

"A couple of hours. You?"

"I'm not great at sleeping. Last night, the whole 'Hey, how about leaving your sisters and going on a quest to fight a dragon' thing got in my head a little."

Callista wanted to start peppering her with questions, but every time the little voice in her head plucked one from the long list, all she could hear was the younger her being an annoying pest. So, she kicked at the horse and said, "Let's get this day started," and shot out down the road like a bolt.

They wouldn't gallop for too far, as it's best not to burn the horses out this early, but to start their day, it let them and their mounts knock out the cobwebs.

When they got to the first turn, Callista still out in front, she slowed to a walk.

"You've gotten better at riding. When did you grow up?" Trilina asked.

"I think it was this week. Have you ever been chased by a fire spider?"

"No. I've not been chased by anything. What did you do?"

Callista told the story of their adventures in the cave in great detail, some of which had been covered the night before, but Trilina didn't seem to mind. It was the first time Callista could recall her cousin asking her about something. It made pretending to be an equal easier.

When the story finished, Trilina asked, "Were you scared?"

She considered her answer. Bravado seemed misplaced, as Trilina was family. Callista said, "It was terrifying, the first time in the cave, but when we went back, I wasn't as nervous."

They walked on for a while and then did a stretch of trotting. The horses were doing well and seemed eager to pick up the pace.

Callista talked about the training Kal had been

giving her. As it was getting about time to dismount and let the animals have a bit of time to graze, she asked the question she'd been thinking about all morning, "How did you become a mage?"

Trilina didn't answer for a while.

Callista almost told her to forget it and that she was sorry for prying, but she could tell her cousin was looking for the right words.

"When Mom died, she left each of us letters. They were similar except for the post-script, which we were not supposed to share with anyone, even each other. Mom told me where to find a chest with all these books in it.

"I was so sad at the time, what with losing her and Dad, and realizing that I had to run the farm, so when I found all these books with letters and instructions from Mom, I did as I was told.

"She said on the very first page that I needed to read the first book in order, slowly and not to skim. By the end, I would understand. That's how it started.

"At first, she just gave me general advice on what to do to keep the farm and to protect my sisters. Then one day, I should mention, that I was supposed to read only one per day, and each entry had a date on it. Not the date it was written, but the day I was to read it. Mom knew they were going to die."

Callista hung on every word. "And she couldn't stop it?"

"Honestly, I don't know if she couldn't or wouldn't. She had a vision of the future that was clearer than I remember the past. Anyway, on one day she explained about her visions. She told me I wouldn't believe her, and I didn't. Then she said I'd see three owls that day. By the time I had read the post, I'd already seen one. The moment I finished the line about the owls, another flew up and landed on top of the barn. It gave a single hoot. Just before sunset, I saw the third.

"In the years we had lived there, I'd never seen an owl. I didn't know what it meant. I guess I still don't, but Mom had seen it, written about it, and just as she had intended, made me believe.

"So, on our birthday last year, Mom told me I was to be a mage. I've been studying ever since."

Callista had been listening to her cousin intently, and neither had noticed that riders stalked them from behind right away. Figures in dark cloaks, with black eyes, and fingers wrapped around knives, seemed to be waiting for their chance.

They reached the top of a hill and slowed.

Trilina pointed toward the small grove of trees at the base of the long hill they'd just climbed. "Did you see that?"

They both looked. Callista said, "I don't see anything."

"I think we should go. Once we're over the hill, then we…"

Her plan to try to gain some distance on whatever she thought was back there became a moot point as the six horsemen flew out from their cover and rode like the wind.

"Ride!" Trilina shouted.

Their horses sensed the danger. They both bolted down the hill. When they got to the bottom and looked back, the riders were gaining on them.

Her horse didn't need her to tell it what to do. Callista dropped the reins and grabbed her bow from around her shoulders, pulled an arrow, and tried to nock it, but she couldn't. The violence of the horse galloping at full-speed was too much, and even if she had been able to fire, she doubted she could have hit anything. She put the arrow back and grabbed the reins again.

They rode as hard as they could. When they got to the bridge crossing the river, Trilina pulled up, turned the horse back toward the riders and cast the summoning spell. A massive wolf, more substantial than the one she had summoned before, leapt out of a flash of light and landed in the center of the bridge.

When Callista saw her cousin stopped, she yanked the reins, and her horse slid to a stop. She turned the horse around, grabbed the bow, nocked an arrow and fired it at the lead rider who was still one hundred meters off. The arrow flew straight, but the lead rider leaned to the right, and it was a miss. She fired two more arrows in quick succession. The first was to the left, and though it missed the rider she was aiming at, it struck the one furthest back in the shoulder. The second one missed completely. They kept coming.

The summoned wolf took off for the approaching riders. It leapt at the lead rider. Its fangs sunk into an arm, tearing the rider from its mount.

Callista cast another spell, and the rider with the

arrow in its shoulder veered off the road and stopped. Wildly he seemed to be fighting some unknown foe.

Trilina swung her horse back around. She dug her heels into its side, and the beast broke into a gallop. Callista fired one more arrow and followed without waiting to see if it landed.

Callista's heart was pounding. This attack wasn't like the spiders, where she knew that safety was within reach. They were exposed with nowhere to hide. A knife whizzed past her ear.

The lead rider of the four who remained was just two lengths back.

They kept riding.

Trilina, just ahead of her cousin, cast another spell, and a second wolf landed in the road right at the feet of the first rider, tripping the horse, sending the rider flying. A second rider's horse went down. The two remaining veered around the fallen beasts which put them four lengths back.

One of the riders loosed an arrow that struck Trilina in the shoulder. She cried out in pain.

Seeing the arrow in her cousin caused something to click inside Callista. Time seemed to slow. She sensed her heart rate dropping, and suddenly the gait of the horse didn't feel as rough. She pulled her bow and an arrow. Her fingers nocked it deftly.

The riders were back to within less than a length. Twisting in the saddle, Callista loosed the arrow and struck the rider right through the eye. He died before he hit the ground.

As she reached for another arrow, a knife lodged

into her left shoulder, and she dropped the bow.

Still the hooded figured on its black stallion thundered toward her. The pain was intense, but the feeling of time having slowed remained. Callista was not panicked.

The one remaining threat pulled up beside her on the right. She saw the bandit's arm reach back over his shoulder to draw the sword.

There wasn't a moment of hesitation. Callista jerked the reins with all the strength of her left arm, and her horse broke from its gallop. In one fluid motion, she pulled the knife from her shoulder and arched her arm out to the side, striking the hooded man in the chest, his arm still drawing the sword.

The blade went straight into his heart, and he died instantly.

Trilina pulled her horse up and swung around and back to Callista. Blood poured from their respective wounds.

Behind them, the two summoned wolves were tearing at flesh. The attacker who had been hit with the ghost illusion spell was riding away.

Callista said, "I've got bandages."

Trilina shook her head. "I could only remember two spells," she said and looked down at the hooded man lying on the road with the knife in his chest. "They don't look like bandits."

"I have no idea," Callista said as she got off her horse and started digging through the saddle bag and continued, "but we sure showed them they shouldn't pick on women riding alone."

A smile flashed on Trilina's face. "That was an impressive move. He never saw it coming."

Callista handed the bandages to her cousin. "If you could wrap up my shoulder, I should be in good enough shape to deal with that arrow in your back."

Trilina looked over her shoulder. "Yes, it's not a good look for me."

Callista laughed, bent down, pulled the dagger from the dead rider, and said, "I'm keeping this." And then she added, "It feels strange in my hand. Check it out; do you feel that?" She flipped the blade in the air, grabbed the tip, and held it out for Trilina.

Trilina took it. Held it for a moment and said, "Yes, it seems as if it has its own power. It must have some magical component," she said and then grimaced. "Let's figure this out later and get ourselves patched up first."

They got to work. While the horses grazed in the field just off the road, Trilina put the bandage on Callista's shoulder after applying healing balm.

Callista then carefully removed the arrow, inspected it for signs of poison, found none, and then marveled at the craftsmanship. "This is a fine arrow."

"I'm glad you like your shiny new arrow. Now, about that healing?"

"Oh, sorry," she said, with a little bit of a giggle. "Surviving an ambush is scary at first, but winning the day is pretty exciting."

"You're right about that, but if I had lost you, well…" Trilina let her words trail off.

Callista hugged her cousin.

Trilina said, "But we did it. My first fight turned out alright, though I think we got a bit lucky."

Callista applied the balm, gave her a potion to drink, and wrapped a banding over the wound. "You should be back to nearly good as new once the potion takes effect in a few minutes."

"I can feel it healing. It's like the tissue is weaving itself back together. Did you make this potion?"

"Yes, Gran taught me."

"Good stuff, even better than our brandy, which, if I'm not mistaken, I think I have a bottle of here in my saddle bag. A quick shot, and we get back on our way, okay?"

Callista said, "Are you kidding? I'm going to see what other things this guy and his friends might have on him," kneeling by the body and beginning her search. She found two more knives with the same magic feel. The sword was nice but didn't appear to be special beyond the fine craftsmanship. There was a small bag of fifteen gold coins which she offered to share, but Trilina told her to keep it.

They walked up the road and dug through the other bodies. It was a pretty good haul, as each man had a few of the daggers. There were a total of three amulets and four rings on the bodies. The total gold was eight more coins and an additional twenty silver. The bow of the archer had the same magic feel, but Callista couldn't draw it. Also, the archer had a nice pair of gloves. She grabbed those, too. There were nineteen of the arrows in his quiver, which she took as well.

The entire haul fit nicely in the saddlebags of two of the riders' horses. They were impressive beasts, one ink black and the other a speckled gray, and though it would slow them down to bring them along, they would still make it to Peja. The next day, these two would help them get to the farm more quickly. Trilina guessed they were Percherons, because of their incredible strength and speed.

The last thing they went through was the saddle bag of the first rider's horse taken down by the wolf back at the bridge. In it, they found a letter written in a language neither could read and two scrolls.

Callista found the bow she had dropped and slung it over her shoulder. With that, they were done.

The two women walked back to their horses leading the Percherons. Both their mounts were still covered in sweat and dirt but seemed fine. Callista pulled four apples from her saddlebag and gave one to each of the horses. Their new horses were especially appreciative of the treat and the pats on the nose.

The sun was getting low. They still had several hours of riding ahead of them, but each had a sense of a deep inner growth at having survived the day.

CHAPTER TWENTY-FOUR

After greeting each one of her staff by name, asking about their children, and spending an hour looking over the books with the manager, Trilina found Callista in the kitchen eating a beef pie.

"Your cook is incredible. Have you tasted her beef pie?"

Trilina laughed. "Yes, she's a master and the reason the farm never loses employees. Nobody could live without her *pumpes*. When we get back from wherever this adventure leads us, I'll have her whip up some. They'll make your mouth sing."

"Then we better kill that dragon quickly."

The cook slid a plate of beef pie in front of Trilina, who sat down and dug in. She waited until the cook had left and whispered, "There's something we need to go find. Mom mentioned that she'd hidden some things for me, and that one day I'd be needing them, but not to find the chest until I was about to go on an adventure. I've been wondering what she meant by an 'adventure' for years."

Taking a big bite, then chewing it and making an audible sound of dining ecstasy, Callista swallowed and said, "So, you're saying that after dinner we're going on a treasure hunt."

"Yes."

"I'm in."

The cousins finished their meat pies, thanked the cook, and headed out into the fresh evening air. Trilina grabbed two shovels from the barn, and off they went toward the forest.

"Are we going to need torches? It will be dark soon."

"It wouldn't have helped back on the road, but I've got an interesting spell. I'll show you once we're in the woods."

They walked and chatted, mostly about the farm, and what it was like to have built such an operation. Callista found every story fascinating. When they got to a path that had been worn by deer, Trilina stopped. The sun was down, and it was time to make some light.

She picked up two branches, about four centimeters in diameter, and broke off all the smaller branches until she had two sticks about the length of their forearms. With her knife she carved a small notch in each one, then in a voice that sounded like monks chanting, she said, *"Lux noctis linga"* and the first notch she'd carved out began to glow a bright white light.

Callista clapped. "That's impressive."

"Wait, there's more. Check this out, if I touch it to the other torch, see what happens?"

The notch on the second one took the light. "I could carve notches on trees around a campfire and light them all up, without actually burning the trees."

"Can I try?"

Trilina explained how she made her voice vibrate a certain way and that it had taken a lot of practice.

Callista gave it a try without success. She tried two more times before saying, "We'll have plenty of time for you to teach me on the road. Let's find that treasure."

They walked down the path as it wound its way through the woods. It crossed a dry creek, and went up a steep embankment. After a long curve, an old stone hut, weathered by time, lay up ahead.

Trilina said, "It's supposed to be buried near the northwest corner."

"How are we going to tell which way is northwest in the dark? I can't even see the sky through the trees."

"I've been out here a hundred times, thinking I wanted to dig it up, but resisting the urge. I know where to dig."

They took turns. The ground was hard, and there were roots from nearby trees that made the digging a challenge. Down about one meter, Trilina finally hit something.

The chest was more massive than they had anticipated, and they had to dig a bigger hole. When

Callista and Trilina finally got enough space that they could reach their hands down and try to lift it out, it was too heavy.

Trilina cursed her mother.

They dug more space on the sides, and once they could get their feet into the hole, both of them hoisted the chest up and out.

It wasn't locked.

On top, there was a brown leather book with her mother's name on it. The book looked ancient, and the lettering seemed to glow. It sat on top of a silk robe of bold red with a gold dragon on the back and strange stitching of glyphs all around the sleeves. Under the robe, a wooden box with inlays of more glyphs. Below that was another robe, this one blue, with silver stitching, and like before, there was another wooden box.

Callista marveled at the find. "This is incredible."

"I know. Mom made up for all the missed birthdays."

Below the second box were a burlap sack and a hand-written note.

Dear Trilina,

Packing up all of these things for your future was hard. Your father tried to comfort me. He brought wine, and before the bottle was empty, we were laughing like on our first date.

This is likely the last thing I'll be writing to you. You'll have discovered the books, but this is the night before we left, to, well...you know.

Trilina…Don't be sad.

There might have been more than one bottle.

You remember that time at your aunt's when we got a little out of control and laughed all night. You and your sisters kept complaining. It was like that.

The point is, your father made me include the burlap sack. He said you wouldn't bring anything to carry all of this home. It's not magical or anything, but know that your father was thinking of you always.

You'll notice there's quite a lot in here. Most of it you won't be able to use for many years. That's fine, keep following the book and do the best you can to keep you and your sisters safe.

Your father says, don't forget to feed the cows.

He's had more wine than me, but he did most of the digging, so it's only fair.

Love,

Mom and Dad.

P.S. I know it seems like I can see every bit of the future, but please know that I can't. The book is not a complete vision of your whole life; there will be dangers and triumphs that were beyond my powers to scry.

P.P.S. Hug your sisters and tell them we love them.

Trilina wiped the tears from her eyes. "I know she told me not to, but that was so like Mom and Dad to get drunk the night before they were to die."

"It's what I'd do."

Trilina laughed. "Me too. Let's put all the stuff in dad's burlap sack and sort it out later."

"I hope there's some more of that meat pie left. This was brutal."

The very last piece of treasure was a description of the items Trilina should be able to use as a new mage. She folded up that piece of paper, put it in her pocket, and led her cousin out of the woods.

When they got back to the house, both were too tired to spend time figuring out what everything was in the chest. Trilina packed away the first few items on the list.

Callista headed off to bed, while Trilina gave a few parting instructions for the manager about the farm. She told him she'd be gone for a while and to keep things running. Also, she had his smartest assistant pack to leave with them to take her place keeping books at the Third Eye.

It was the last thing to put in order before she laid down to get some rest. The trip had been exhausting. Trilina worried about whether there would be more danger on the return trip. Having the extra man with them did make her feel better. He was good with a sword. She needed her rest. But, on this night, her sleep was filled with nightmares, unlike anything she'd ever known. Maybe this was another sign; maybe their adventure wasn't going to go as they planned.

CHAPTER TWENTY-FIVE

A companionable silence fell between them as they rode. Since Matilda had first earned them a bed and meal at an inn, they'd aimed for a different town each night on their way to the capital and a woman Elora called the silver witch.

Each day the coldness Elora displayed had thawed a little. In part, thanks to Matilda and, in part, thanks to the progress they made.

The horses he'd purchased were serving them well. A good night's rest in a stable at each inn was giving them a hardiness Rhysdan hadn't expected. He didn't know how badly they must have fared before he purchased them, but it was clear he'd bought them from someone he shouldn't have trusted. No doubt his savings would be gone.

Perhaps one more adventure was worth it, he thought. *Assuming we all live to talk about fighting off a dragon.*

"How far is the next inn?" Matilda asked. It was still early afternoon, but she let out a yawn as she spoke.

She'd worked her magic each night, begged by her listeners to keep playing until the early hours of the morning. It made the innkeeper happy. The money kept coming in as long as the drinks flowed, but it was taking its toll on her.

Did magic come at a cost? Did she even know she might be draining herself of a resource?

Rhysdan had these thoughts every time they stopped for the night. So far, he'd kept them to himself, but he couldn't any longer.

"Where did you learn to play, Matilda?" As he spoke, he noticed Elora shooting him a look, making it clear she was considering stabbing him to shut him up.

I'm considering it too, love, he thought. *But I've begun now.*

"My father," she replied, not picking up on anything but an interested curiosity.

"Did he play as well as you?"

"Better. This one time it was so good he stopped a camp full of men arguing. Probably stopped a fight. By the time he'd finished the song they were all sitting around him."

Rhysdan nodded. He could imagine it. It wasn't a far cry from what he'd seen her do.

"Sometimes he'd play for mother too, but it used to make her even angrier if he tried to when they were arguing. Not that they argued much…" Matilda trailed off, the smile gone from her face.

Wincing, Rhysdan almost didn't continue. Hurting the lass by making her miss her parents wasn't his intention, but someone had to keep an eye out for her and be responsible.

"Sounds like he was a powerful mage too," he blurted.

Matilda whipped her head around to look at him, her eyes wide. It was evident the thought hadn't occurred to her at all.

"Normal people don't play like that."

"They don't?"

"No." Elora shook her head again, but this time her voice was soft. "You and your father put a spell on people when you play. I've suspected for a while that it's what drew me to you when we met. I was already slowing when I saw you."

"You were? I thought you were going to run me down."

"No. I felt compelled to stop for you. You called me to you with your playing. And you've used your magic to win us favor since."

Matilda frowned, not replying until her eyes lit up. She asked, "Could it be the lute?"

Rhysdan felt his heart break a little as he shook his head.

"I don't think so, Matilda." Elora gave her a gentle smile, but she didn't return it.

"But you don't know. Not for sure. It might not be me at all. My father might have had the lute enchanted or something. He never usually let it out of his sight.

That's how I knew he was taken."

Matilda kept shaking her head; her words were clipped and aggressive.

"You shot steam at a soldier, didn't you?"

Once more Rhysdan winced. *Easy, Elora. The lass is scared and wields magic—not a good combination.* But Elora didn't appear to notice the change in Matilda.

"You can do magic, and you need to learn to control it. That's why I…"

"No! You're not my parent. And I'm not a child anyway. I've never done magic, and neither has my father. We're just good at playing."

"Matilda! You can't deny what you've done and bury your head in the sand."

She let out a growl and dug her heels into the flanks of her mount. Before either Rhysdan or Elora could react, her horse was off, running into the trees to one side of them.

"Matilda, don't be so stupid," Elora yelled as Rhysdan sighed.

She didn't respond, ignoring them as her horse carried her off into the distance. The trees obscured their view, and soon they could only hear the sound of her horse as it brushed past bushes and crunched the fallen leaves.

That went well. Should have waited till Matilda was more comfortable with the idea of doing magic.

"Urrggh. Of all the irresponsible things to do! Is she trying to get herself killed?"

"She's young and scared," Rhysdan said, despite sharing some of Elora's frustration.

"Scared of what? She's got a great gift if she'd learn how to control it."

"Can't blame the lass for wanting to be normal. It might be a gift in your eyes, but not everyone sees it that way. It can also be a burden." He watched Elora deflate, calm enough to think about it from Matilda's point of view again.

"We'd best find her before she gets hurt."

"Agreed."

***

When Matilda's horse slowed, so did her heart rate. For a few minutes, she'd ridden hard, wanting to get away from Elora and Rhysdan and their accusations. It was a dangerous pace in such a closed in wood, and the mare soon protested, bucked a few times and refused to go faster again.

At first, Matilda considered getting off the horse and running, but her sense returned. It was bad enough she'd fled the way she had. After doing the same to her parents and returning to find them gone, she should have learned her lesson.

With a sigh, she stopped the horse. She wasn't ready to head back to the road and find the others yet, but she had already put enough distance between them.

Was she a mage? It was a question that had haunted her since escaping from Aldrei's camp. Every time she tried to sleep her mind filled with nightmares. She didn't want powers.

But Rhysdan's words kept coming to mind. Ordinary people couldn't play like her and her father.

She'd always believed her father was that good. That practice and a life dedicated to it had made him so proficient that people would stop what they were doing, even if they were about to draw swords on each other.

Had he been wielding magic? Could she do the same thing?

Matilda knew there was only one way to find out.

Sitting on the ground beside her horse, she readied her lute and concentrated. Focusing on how she'd felt when Elora had first come riding up, Matilda began to play the same tune.

It only took a few seconds for a pair of wood pigeons to settle on a nearby branch. Not long after that, a squirrel appeared, running up to a log a few feet away. Perching on top, it washed its face with its paws. They came because her music called to them.

Matilda kept playing.

***

Rhysdan led his horse by the reins, studying the ground beside Elora when he felt an inexplicable tug in one direction.

"You feel that?" he asked Elora. She tilted her head to the side as if listening.

"I think she's playing."

"Helping us find her?"

"Or testing her magic. Either way, it's a good sign."

"As long as she's only calling us to her," Rhysdan said as he spotted a hideout a bandit might use. There were bootprints in the dirt around it, and the leaves which generally covered the entrance from prying eyes were pushed to one side.

When was someone last here? Are they heading towards Matilda as well, drawn by her music?

"Hurry," he said when he saw the smoking remains of a wood fire a few hundred meters further on.

They weren't alone in the forest.

Elora didn't need to be told twice to pick up the pace, both of them trusting the instinct they felt to guide them to Matilda until they could hear the sound of her strumming out a gentle forlorn tune.

It made him think of a forest longing for summer while in the depths of winter.

He jogged on, letting go of the horse to get there faster. Elora did the same and drew her sword. They crashed through the trees until they spotted Matilda.

She sat on a log, looking calm even though the six men of various ages and sizes stood around her. Her eyes flicked to Rhysdan only briefly as her fingers continued her tune.

"Look, lads, the girl's not alone," the largest man said. He had a smug grin on his face yet one hand rested on the hilt of his sword

"I did tell you I wasn't," Matilda said. The tune she played changed subtly. Rhysdan found himself calming, relaxing despite the danger.

"Looks like you're all trespassing on our land. I'm in a good mood today, so we'll let you make an offer to pay our toll. Then the three of you can leave."

Rhysdan frowned. They had nothing of value.

"You can see we don't have anything," Elora replied, lifting her sword point just a little. "We'll get off your land right away. Come on, Matilda."

Somehow Matilda managed to stand and keep playing, but as she took a step towards Elora, the lead bandit drew his sword.

"I think we'll keep the instrument you've been playing so sweetly, and we'll have anything else you possess." He pointed his blade at her, but instead of handing over the instrument she frowned and kept playing. The mood shifted again, but it had an edge of panic to it, and the rest of the men drew their swords.

"She's keeping the lute, and she's coming with us," Rhysdan said, edging closer to her, wanting to get between her and danger. Before he could, the calmness Matilda had been creating vanished, and one of the men lunged at her. She squealed as she pulled the lute out of reach and stretched out her hand as she had at the soldier in the camp.

Nothing happened.

With the music gone the men laughed and advanced.

"Stop!" Matilda yelled, trying to sound commanding and failing. "I'm a powerful mage. Come any closer, and I'll blast you all."

They paused, looking to their leader, but he bellowed his laughter.

"She's not lying," Rhysdan said. "She's still learning to control it, but she's telling you the truth. And either way," he lifted his sword and took another step forward, "she's under my protection, and she's not handing you that lute."

"What exactly are you going to do to stop me taking it, old man? Do you think you can best all six of us?"

No, he thought. *I can't, but that won't stop me trying.*

Before he could say yes, Elora laughed. A bright sound in the tense atmosphere.

"You men think you're so clever and skilled." Elora pointed her sword at the leader. "I challenge you to a duel. We win, we all leave with the instrument. You win, and you get to keep the lute and our horses."

Rhysdan shook his head. Some protector he was if he let Elora fight this battle. But the bandit leader beat him to uttering anything.

"You challenge me? Why would I accept when we can take all that anyway?"

"Oh come on, don't tell me you're afraid of dueling with a woman, are you?"

The leader laughed again.

"All right then, you have your duel."

"Elora?" Rhysdan said, stepping up to her as the rest of the men lowered their weapons. The look she gave him stopped him from voicing anything else.

"Make sure Matilda gets where she needs to, and you find Marl. They need to know what you and she have seen."

Matilda, eyes wide, hurried over to his side, her lute back in the usual place. No one stopped her this time.

This isn't going to work. Even if Elora wins, they'll attack as soon as she's bested their leader.

"Get ready to run," he whispered to Matilda as Elora gave him one last glance and stepped forward. The leader gave her a nod and a quick salute with his sword. It was all the warning she got.

He lunged.

Barely moving, she deflected it. The same happened when he tried to strike again, each responsive movement from her so fast her blade blurred.

While he attacked, she parried until he shifted position, coming in closer to try and find a weak spot. As he slashed with his blade again, she blocked it and flicked her wrist just enough to catch the guard. It yanked the weapon out of his hand and sent it spinning away.

Before Rhysdan could blink, Elora had her sword tip at the bandit's throat.

"There," she said. "I win. Now we'll be on our way."

"Very well," he replied, growling the last part. He clenched both fists but kept them at his sides.

Rhysdan took Matilda's hand and started to lead her away while Elora kept her position.

"I must admit, I considered sending you to meet whichever god you might worship," Elora said, keeping the bandit in place. "But I've decided not to. Aldrei is back. If you value your lives, you'll stop this silliness and go back to whatever village you lived in before. They'll need your swords."

Elora stepped back, her eyes not leaving the bandit

leader. His eyes blazed, and he gritted his teeth, but the bandit leader didn't move.

Although Elora kept her outside appearance calm when Rhysdan caught her gaze it was full of concern. She strode towards him, encouraging them on ahead of her.

"They're getting away, boss," one of the other men said, but the trio didn't stop or look back.

"I gave them my word," the leader said. Matilda looked behind and hesitated.

"Don't stop, lass. We're not safe yet."

But Matilda stopped, her eyes going wide.

"Look out!" she yelled, giving him a shove with one hand. The other snapped out towards the bandits.

As he reeled sideways, he spun himself, catching a tree branch to keep from falling over. Air rushed together into a small tornado, hitting a flying dagger as it sailed through the air towards him.

The small blade clattered away.

Matilda's whirlwind carried on, picking up leaves, dust, and small twigs.

The men yelped as the debris pelted them. It took the remaining desire to fight out of them. They turned and fled, leaving the trio of travelers alone.

After all the commotion the forest seemed eerily quiet, the only sound Matilda's tired gasps for breath. Elora slipped an arm around her waist, keeping her from falling over.

Some protector I am, he thought. They both did the saving.

"You need to teach me those fancy moves of

yours, Elora," he said, instead of voicing his actual thoughts.

She grinned and nodded, sheathing her sword.

"Good. I'll see if I can find our horses. Don't much want to be here when those fellas return."

"I can get them to come back," Matilda said, reaching for her lute. "The horses, I mean."

Elora frowned but helped her sit.

"Are you sure, lass? You don't look your usual sunny self."

She nodded, meeting his eyes, "We might have to sleep under the stars tonight to give me a rest from using magic, but we need our horses either way."

It was a good point.

Sitting nearby, he watched as she played the same tune they'd heard earlier. Within seconds he felt drawn to her, wanting to sit and listen forever.

Other animals started to appear until he spotted all three of their horses picking their way through the trees.

At first neither he or Elora moved, listening in a sort of trance. Matilda's finger slipped, playing a jarring note, and the moment ended, all the animals and humans blinking from their daze.

Getting to his feet, he hurried over to secure the horses. It was more than time to get back on the road.

"Sorry for running," Matilda said as she swung into the saddle.

"I'm sorry for pushing you," Elora replied. "I just wanted you to understand that some of us would give almost anything to have the gift you possess."

Matilda nodded. "I think I'd like to go see your friend now."

"A day or two's ride, and we'll be there." Elora steered her mare towards the road, and Matilda tucked in behind, leaving Rhysdan to bring up the rear.

Rhysdan sighed. He knew the adventure was beginning.

CHAPTER TWENTY-SIX

Everyone sensed it. The unspoken reality of the continuing journey was real. Kal decided the party would leave the next morning. One more day to get weapons sharpened, to make plans, and to prepare supplies.

Late into the night, Marl, Kal, and Elora debated about where to begin the search. Elora had heard of a couple of sightings of the dragon, and they were vast distances apart along the massive wall of Fog. They agreed that the most logical place to start looking was at the sighting near Tarnton Baston, as it was the closest sighting to where Elora had found the camp of worshipers.

Much time was spent deliberating how to deal with the followers who appeared to be brainwashed or under some spell. There was also the matter of Matilda's parents, who may be part of the group.

It would take four days to get to the baston. They could rest along the way in Mossbrook and Freyburn. After some discussion and a bit of arguing, Marl decided it was best to take the northern split in the road outside of Freyburn and go through Dobtin. They wanted to avoid as much battle as possible while they gathered information.

Now, in the light of their last day before heading out, the mood was solemn. Callista had gotten up before Kal, and without him asking, had done a dozen sets of pulling his bow and working on her strength. Trilina, who hadn't slept well, had the two books she'd brought with her and was trying to figure out how to use the wand her mother had told her would be her first. It wasn't going well.

Marl, helping Raina with the fire, looked at Trilina and said, "I don't know about her. What sort of mage doesn't know how to use their wand?"

"She'll be fine. It's her focus, but Trilina is bright, she'll get there. And when she does, you'll be thankful she's on your side."

"It's a young group. They lack experience. What's going to happen when they meet Aldrei? He's older now and likely has his breath. I remember the first dragon that I faced, that bastard Tudeg, with his ice-needle breath. A lot of men died that day. And I was scared shitless."

"Yes, but you still, despite being younger than Trilina, leaped on the dragon's neck and fought like a rabid wolf until it threw you and flew off, never to be seen again. What makes you think this young group won't rise to the occasion just as you did?"

Marl looked her in the eyes and said, "Because they're all a lot smarter than me."

Raina pointed at the young women, who had now been joined by Matilda, who seemed to be fascinated by Trilina's efforts to unlock the mysteries of her wand. "They are hungry to learn."

"I'm sure that Aldrei is just as hungry…for a snack. Do you know how much a dragon of that age eats?"

"No idea, but I know how much you lot eat, so go check on the chickens, and let's see what we have for breakfast."

Marl sighed. She hadn't alleviated his fears, but she did put together a good feed, so he went off to discuss his concerns with the chickens.

At the coop he found Jenson. Still recovering from the poison, he was able to move around a bit. "How are you feeling?"

"Like a freeloader. I thought I'd feed the chickens."

"Raina won't admit it; I know she's glad you're here. I have a special task for you."

"Anything."

"Even if you feel strong enough, hang around and keep an eye on her."

"You don't want me to try to catch up with you?"

"Even if you got strong enough to ride, which I think is a ways off, I don't think you'd have much strength behind your sword. But, knowing you're here, well, that's one thing I won't have to worry about."

Jenson nodded. "And what are the other things on

your mind?"

"The dragon is six years older. If he hasn't gotten his breath, well, we shouldn't have any problems. Wasting these last two weeks, running around, when every day he gets one day older, that's got me worried. And the team isn't too seasoned."

"Why not let the king's army take care of it?"

Marl didn't talk for a long time. He grabbed a handful of corn and threw it around the yard for the hens, trying to find the right words. "I can't explain it, really, but there's been an open wound in my soul that won't heal up. Maybe it's stupid, but if I put down the beast once and for all, well, maybe…" His voice trailed off.

Jenson seemed to understand.

When the chickens were fed, Jenson went back to the cottage to lie down.

Marl found his whetstone and sharpened his sword, for about the twentieth time over the last few days.

CHAPTER TWENTY-SEVEN

Marl stood on the porch. The gathered party looked up at him. He saw eagerness in their eyes, and a fair amount of tension in their postures. Nobody thought this was going to be easy, and each carried a reason to be nervous.

The horses were ready, saddlebags packed, and the weather looked to be in their favor, as there wasn't a cloud in the sky. Even Kal looked brighter eyed than usual.

Raina sat on the bench with Jenson, who had made it out of bed to wish them well.

With practiced confidence that comes with years of soldiering, Marl said, "We travel to Tarnton Baston, through Mossbrook, Freyburn, and we've decided to take the northern route through Dobtin. It should take us three days to Dobtin and then Tarnton Baston will be a comfortable ride out on the fourth.

"Along the way, we keep our eyes peeled. I'm not concerned about bandits because, far and wide, Kal is known to have terrible morning breath."

Nobody had expected a laugh line, except Elora, who went with an eye roll but smiled nonetheless.

"These are going to be the hardest days of your lives. The dragon will try to kill you. He will try to kill us all. We must be vigilant for any signs. Claw marks on trees, a burnt patch, or a pile of half-eaten bodies."

He hadn't intended to get a laugh on the last line. Marl had seen plenty of dragon victims, and often they were only parts. He brushed past the unintentional moment of levity, as he didn't want to lose the tone. This was serious business.

"For the next three days, I don't anticipate much trouble. As we ride, we need to consider how a battle might go. The more each of you can envision trouble, the better we will be as a team. Make no mistake about it: this will be a team effort. If not, well, none of us will likely return."

This last line hit the mark.

He had fought with brave soldiers. Marl knew when their minds were right. His team was ready to go.

"Callista, give your gran a kiss. We've got a dragon to hunt."

CHAPTER TWENTY-EIGHT

He left last as his team of six other adventurers headed out. Marl stopped just before they entered the woods, turned back and caught Raina's look. The unease in his gut seemed to settle.

Despite his speech, Marl could see the younger members of the group could not help but show excitement in a way he and his old friends had long since dismissed as folly. Callista, Matilda, and Trilina rode up ahead.

Marl, who hadn't gotten to know much about Rhysdan, found out where he was from. He'd grown up in a village to the north by the name of Dubney, near Rye Baston. His parents had farmed, mostly grains, but had a few pigs, goats, and chickens. He was big for his age and took to fighting. At eighteen he'd set out with friends to find their riches. Less than a year later his three best mates were dead, and he settled in the south, working for a while on the docks in Wexstone.

As Marl listened, he noted how Rhysdan didn't tell the tale with regret. It was just an account of where he'd been in life. They talked about their blades for a while, as men are wont to do, and even some of their battle scars. He seemed a competent sword, who had also trained with a battle axe and halberd, though he hadn't used either in years.

Elora and Kal rode behind them, getting caught up.

He hadn't noticed how far ahead Callista, Matilda, and Trilina had gotten until they stopped and dismounted.

Marl broke into a gallop and came up fast, ready for a problem, but there was just an old woman sitting in the ditch with her knees up to her chest. The rest of the party was right behind.

Trilina, who was knelt by the woman, looked up at Marl and said, "She won't say what happened. Just keeps rocking back and forth."

Marl climbed down off his horse and said in a soft voice, "Would you let us help you?"

The woman looked up and shook her head back and forth violently.

Elora pulled Marl aside and said, "Let me talk to her."

With no objection, she sat down across from the woman and asked, "Did someone or something hurt you?"

With less vigor than before, she nodded back and

forth and then looked down at her knees.

Elora asked, "Did something frighten you? Did you see a dragon?"

The woman started rocking again.

"Please let us help you."

No response.

One by one they tried to get the poor woman to talk or get out of the ditch or to tell them where she lived.

Finally, Matilda, who had been standing on the road silently, began to play. The melody wove its magic, and the old woman stopped rocking. She looked up at Matilda and said, "You done wipe the fear right out of my chest."

Matilda stopped playing and asked, "Do you live near her?"

The woman sat still and thought for a bit. She stood up and looked all around and then pointed off to the east. "My cousins live just over yonder. I'll be fine."

Marl asked, "Are you sure?"

"Yes, but I can tell you, that giant red dragon put an awful fright into me."

Glances back and forth, then Marl said, "Where did you see it?"

The woman just pointed up.

"Which way did it go?"

She shrugged.

Marl persisted, "Which way did it come from?"

"Sorry, I don't remember. My head is all fuzzy."

A brief discussion about what to do with the

woman resulted in Elora and Kal volunteering to see her to her cousin's safely and then catch up.

Marl pointed on the map to where he planned to camp, just on the other side of Mossbrook.

The group watched as Kal hoisted up the woman onto the back of his horse, and the three of them rode off in the direction she pointed.

It made Marl uneasy to see the party separated again. Now down two members, if they came across Aldrei, being without Elora's sword and Kal's bow could spell disaster. *Better to keep everyone together,* he thought, *but what could they do? Leaving her out here all alone, well that wasn't an option.*

***

For almost an hour they rode. The woman telling him where to go, which road to take, and always pointing forward. Kal was beginning to regret their kindness, but finally, it seemed they were almost there.

She touched his back and said, "Slow down, the path is hard to find."

Kal slowed the horse to a walk. Elora pulled up next to them looking a little annoyed about how far they had gone.

The woman said, "Here, through that patch over there. A trail starts just on the other side."

The horses waded through the bushes and onto an overgrown trail.

"It's just up there, around the bend. I do appreciate this so much. We were much further away than I realized. I'm so very sorry about all this bother."

Elora said nothing.

Kal eased the horse forward and said, "It's our pleasure. We want you to be safe."

The horses rounded the dense growth of trees and on the other side was a surprisingly well-kept home, with nicely maintained flower boxes, a tiny courtyard out front with crushed stone and a birdbath. The roof had fresh straw. The windows were painted blue.

Kal helped the woman off the horse.

"You must come in for a cup of tea," she said, with a twinkle in her eye.

Elora said, "We appreciate it, but we need to get back."

"Oh, don't be silly. I have something for you for all your troubles. It's a powerful magic ring, that may help you on your quest."

Elora started to refuse, but Kal was already getting off his horse. He said, "I'd love a cuppa tea."

The woman seemed to know where everything was in the little house. She had a fire going in no time.

Elora asked, "And you said your cousins live here?"

"Oh yes, they're twins, but are likely off hunting."

Kal pulled out a chair and sat down at the kitchen table. Elora eased herself into the one across from him. She gave him a look. He just shrugged.

When the tea was made, the old woman got out three cups and saucers of extraordinarily fine porcelain. After pouring the tea, she set out some sugar cubes and a silver teaspoon.

Kal took a sip and commented, "It's delicious."

The old woman looked at Elora.

Elora didn't move for a moment, but then plucked two cubes of sugar out and dropped them into her cup. She stirred it slowly.

"Go on then; give it a try."

"I'll let it cool for a bit," Elora said.

Kal took another sip. "Now, you said something about a ring?"

"Oh yes, let me get it," she said, and went to a box on a shelf in the other room. She brought it over. A red wood with a high gloss finish and the carving of a mountain scene in the lid, she opened it and inside were ten rings. She pulled one from the first row, with a red gem, and flipped it over. "I believe this is the one. It helps against Dragon's breath. It won't stop the beast from eating you, but you won't get killed right off, either."

Kal's gaze fixed on the rest of the rings. He seemed like he couldn't pull his eyes away. Then he shook his head. "Wow, this tea has a strong kick to it."

The woman looked at Elora, who still hadn't touched a drop. "Go on, honey, give it a try, you'll like it. It will make you feel better from the long ride."

Elora said, "Kal, I think you're poisoned." She stood, drew her sword and held it to the woman's throat.

She gasped, held the box up, and said, "Take them all."

Elora looked down.

The woman dropped the box, and when it hit the table with a bang, a dark cloud of smoke exploded out from the table and covered them all.

Elora thrust her blade, but the woman was gone. She found her way around the table and Kal was still sitting in the chair, coughing. "Come on; we need to get you outside."

Kal stood, but his legs wobbled.

Outside, the horses were just where they had left them. Elora helped Kal get in the saddle. Before they had even turned to go, the house faded and was gone. This seemed to break the spell on Kal.

He kicked at his horse, and they were off. A few minutes later, they both were on the road back. They were an hour plus behind the rest of the party, but things could have turned out much worse.

Elora said, "I didn't trust that old hag."

"Next time I'll listen to your dirty looks."

"Good man," Elora said and added, "Let's see if we can make up some time."

***

When Kal and Elora made it to camp, there was a stew on the fire. Marl seemed relieved to see them. They pulled Marl aside and told him what had happened. Marl said, "The same thing happened to Callista and me, but it was a rotund old man. Charming, though. He disappeared through some cloud. I followed him, and it was some sort of portal."

Elora shook her head. "There was a big cloud, too,

but we were quick to get away from it. The whole house had been an illusion."

Kal said, "It was, but it was more than that, remember, we went up and down steps to get in the house. It was a real house, but it faded away like an illusion after the old woman was gone."

Marl called over the others and told both stories, for Trilina, Matilda, and Rysdan's benefit. They all agreed that they wouldn't break up the party no matter how much it seemed like the right thing to do.

Kal added. "And no more tea."

CHAPTER TWENTY-NINE

The first few people they talked to hadn't heard of any dragon flying around. They seemed quite bothered by the question, though, and everyone promised to be extra vigilant in watching their kids and loved ones.

By mid-day, the ride had become routine. After lunch, storm clouds rolled in, and soon after that they were slogging through a cold downpour. It reminded Marl of his days as a soldier. He turned to Kal, with a smile that seemed out of place. "Nothing like an adventure, eh mate?"

Kal said, "I don't appreciate your sunny disposition." Elora rode on without comment but smiled.

She reminded Marl of his wife, her sister; she was never one to let a little discomfort slow her down. Elora was serious about life, while her sister saw the humor in everything and lived each day as if it was a blessing.

Rhysdan rode up ahead with the "kids" as he had taken to calling them. He said something, but Marl couldn't hear what. All four up ahead stopped.

Marl pulled up on the reins and asked, "Do you see something?"

Rhysdan pointed over to the left. In a field of wildflowers, there was a black mark cutting across the land about one hundred meters from where they were on the road.

Marl sent Trilina and Kal off to the left of the burn mark and Callista and Elora to the right. "One of you keep your eyes on the sky, and the other keeps an eye on the rest of us. If something happens, we all ride to the threat.

"Circle to the other end of the field and don't get more than about three hundred meters off that burn mark. Rhysdan, Matilda and I will go check it out. See if you can find any tracks that might show someone running away. That will tell us where the attack came from originally."

Callista asked, "Do dragons fly in storms like this?"

Marl said, "No, not usually, unless they're hungry. The low clouds mean that if he's up there and decides to dive, he'll be on us with little warning."

The others rode off. Matilda asked, "Should I be ready to play something?"

Marl said, "Good idea," and he led them off toward the burn mark.

He got down from the saddle and looked at the

ground. *Well, at least I know he's got his breath,* Marl thought, and then looked closer at the width of the burn and the length. It seemed too much for such a young dragon. "See here," he said, taking a moment to teach Matilda and Rhysdan something, "This burn mark and the lack of any claw marks, tells me the dragon was in flight. See how it starts small here," he said pointing to the beginning of the charred patch, "and widens out as it stretches along the ground."

He could see that Matilda and Rhysdan were paying attention. It was also clear by the look in her eyes that Matilda was frightened.

Marl walked along the edge of the charred ground until he found the body. The girth of the shoulders and the height made Marl think it was a mountain of a man. He might have been a farmer because there wasn't any sign of a weapon or armor, or maybe just an unlucky traveler.

Scanning the field, both the other pairs were doing as he asked, riding with one scanning the sky and the other looking for anything helpful. Marl waved, and Trilina on the left waved back, while Elora gave a nod.

Rhysdan got off his horse and said, "Marl, I think I found the tracks."

Marl walked over to take a look. A large set of footprints leading into the charred path seemed to snake away back toward the road. Marl got back on the horse, and they followed them. It was clear that the person had been running first one direction and then the next, as if the dragon had been toying with him. There were at least four abrupt changes. The fact that the body was intact, albeit burnt black, meant Aldrei wasn't feeding, he was having a bit of sport.

Both the other teams were at the far side of the field. Marl gave a piercing whistle and waved at them to return.

When the group was back together, he told them what he had learned, but left out the one detail. Why was the breath so powerful?

Matilda asked, "Should we bury the body?"

Marl said, "If we do that, his family will never find him. When we return home if he's still there, we'll lay him to rest, but for now, we must ride on."

By late afternoon, Marl was beat. Everyone else looked pretty tired, too. The rain had stopped. They should have been to Freyburn but judging from the map they were still a couple of hours away. Nobody objected when Marl suggested they make camp, tend to the horses, and try to get an early night's sleep.

CHAPTER THIRTY

Marl had the team on the road early. It had stormed again in the night, so he hadn't gotten as much rest as he had wanted. He didn't remember it being so hard, this life on the road, six years ago.

As they rode, he thought about Aldrei and did the math on how old he should be again. *Was it just six years?*

He couldn't get past how wide and long the burned swath had been. Usually, from everything he'd learned about dragons, they didn't get that much breath until they were twenty-five to thirty years into adulthood. He wondered if maybe it wasn't the same beast. That thought he would keep to himself, as he didn't need to cause the party any undue worry.

They got to the sleepy little village on the edge of the lake, Freyburn, and it was quiet. *No*, he thought, *it was too quiet.* For this hour of the day, there should be people in the streets, someone working the vegetable stand, signs of life in the little store in the center of town. But as they rode through not a soul could be seen.

Marl broke the party into the same groups as the day before. They would do a thorough search and see if they could figure out where everyone had gone.

As he, Matilda, and Rhysdan rode through the town, he realized he didn't need to go looking. "Matilda, why don't you start playing? If anyone is around, they'll come out."

"Okay," she said, with a bewildered look on her face. "It sure doesn't seem like anyone is around, but I'll do my best."

She played, and Marl sat and listened. When the song finished, the only people who showed up were the others in the party. They had heard Matilda's playing and wondered what was happening.

"Thanks, Matilda, but I don't think anyone is here."

When they got to the far edge of town, though, a tiny doll lay in the middle of the road. *What had happened to the people?* There hadn't been any signs of a fight or struggle that Marl had seen, and none of the others reported anything but empty homes.

It would be another long day on the road.

And because of the fewer than expected kilometers the day before, they wouldn't get close to Dobtin. It would give Marl a lot of time to think.

The others seemed to fall back into their conversations. He heard a few comments of worry, but mostly the younger ones were talking about magic. Marl tried to ignore them. He still preferred fighting with steel.

Hours passed, and Marl couldn't help but notice he hadn't noticed any signs of life, not even so much as a bird. "Kal, have you seen any birds, rabbits, or anything else alive?"

Kal looked back at Marl, shook his head, and said, "No, I haven't, and I've been looking. I thought some fresh game for dinner, might be nice. What do you make of it?"

Elora said, "I don't like it. My guess is the folks of Freyburn have been taken off to the camp."

Marl said, "That's what I thought, but looking on the map, that's got to be one hundred and fifty kilometers from the town." Marl slowed his horse a bit, and Elora and Kal did the same. They let Rhysdan and the others get a little bit ahead of them.

Lowering his voice, Kal asked, "What's worrying you, my friend?"

"I've got a bad sense about this dragon," Marl said, turning his head to the sky.

Elora nodded. "I've been uneasy since getting out of that camp. They weren't just obsessed worshipers; it was as if they were building an army."

Kal scoffed. "An army? From farmers and milkmaids? What could they conquer?"

Elora said, "Don't be so quick to dismiss. Some strange things were going on. Who knows what their plans are, but swords and bows aren't the only way to kill."

Marl shook his head. "There's no honor in…"

Elora cut him off. "Evil has no honor."

Silence, as they all thought about the sort of evil that might be brewing.

Kal sat up in his saddle.

Marl noticed his smile. "Yes?"

"Have you thought about what sort of hoard Aldrei might have hidden away?"

"No, I have not. Every time you get chasing gold, I have to save your butt," Marl said, hoping it would put an end to talk of treasure.

"Hey, if we're going to risk our lives, it's always nice to pick up a bit of coin. I'd love to buy a little land, maybe some chickens, get a wife who knows how to cook."

Marl couldn't help himself; the laugh just made its way up from his belly and popped out. "Elora here is an excellent cook."

Elora looked over at Marl and said, "Don't make me stab you."

Kal said, "Awe come on, Elora, you know you fancy me a bit. Can you cook?"

Now, both Marl and Kal were giving his sister-in-law a hard time. It didn't look like she minded. Marl knew her look when she was about to make you wish you hadn't done what you had done. It was the same look her sister used. He'd rather face a dragon than that look, but there wasn't any sign of it.

Elora said, "I'm going to catch up with the others. With you two in charge, I'm pretty sure our days are numbered."

Kal got in one more crack. "So, you're saying you can't cook?"

She looked back with an entirely different look, and one raised eyebrow, said, "I can cook in ways that you can't handle."

Marl and Kal didn't have an answer for that. They just looked at each other and kept riding without another word.

CHAPTER THIRTY-ONE

Trilina couldn't help but smile at her cousin. They'd been riding together for over a week, and Callista was funny. Now, on day three with the entire party, she, Callista, and Matilda had grown close. Most of their time in the saddle had been a discussion of magic.

At night, by the fire, she'd stayed up late reading from the two books she brought with her. Two days ago, she finally figured out how to fire the wand. It took a higher level of concentration than she imagined. The spells she'd gotten good at, but her mom warned her that to cast with the wand would be more difficult. Each day, since her mother's books mentioned that she was to practice magic, she had devoted time to meditation. When she quieted her mind, much more was possible.

While they rode, she had been trying to teach

Matilda and Callista to cast the summon wolf spell, but neither had been able to make it work. They were trying still, and Trilina said, "I think it may be your minds are too loud."

Matilda asked, "What do you mean by loud?"

"Too many thoughts running through it at one time."

Callista laughed and said, "So, thinking about how sore my butt is, whether gran is okay, will we be eaten by a dragon soon, and trying to call forth a wolf, is a bad idea?"

Trilina laughed. "Yes. I've been practicing quieting my mind for over a year."

"Can you teach us how to practice quieting out minds?" Matilda asked, sounding hopeful.

"I've got a room off the office in the bar. During the mornings, before the lunch crowd, it's quiet. I just sat still and tried to imagine a tiny blue orb in front of my face."

Callista tilted her head. "Why a blue orb?"

"Mom said to picture the first thing that came to me, and when I tried it, that's what popped into my head. I don't see it, but I imagine what it might look like if I did. That's how I began. But, it was easier to quiet my mind in a room without a sound. Mom wrote that I'd need to get good enough that I could quiet it in a battle, with chaos and death all around."

Matilda said, "I don't think I could ever do that; I'd be too frightened."

"Callista can tell you. I struggled when the bandits chased us. I could only cast two spells. I have been practicing a spell to knock a person backward, which I wanted to use to knock the riders off their horses, but it was too hard."

Callista asked, "Can we train our minds while we ride?"

Matilda's head nodded. "Let's try."

Trilina described what she was doing, how she pictured the orb off in the distance down the road, and the way she chased stray thoughts out of her mind when they popped up. "The key is to understand that it doesn't happen right away when you begin. But if you pay attention to how often the other thoughts try to creep in, you'll know when you're getting better as you continue to practice."

Rhysdan, who had been riding to Trilina's right, said, "I'll keep an eye open for trouble."

With that, the three women stopped chatting.

They rode without a word.

Callista cracked first and started to say something, but the moment Trilina heard her voice, she said, "Keep trying, no talking."

Trilina could tell she was improving. Not only did the extra thoughts stay away, but the entire world around her also seemed to fade away. The sound of the light breeze was gone. Horse hooves on the road stopped their clopping. Even time seemed to come to a stop. Then a thought popped into her head, could she do it in battle?

She didn't try to answer that question. Answering it wasn't quieting her mind. Instead, she shoved it out into the nothingness. All that mattered was the silence.

Her mother called it "state of flow" and said that the magic of the world could only flow through her when she could bring the stillness of the mind.

Even remembering her mother's words were disturbing the quiet. She took in a deep breath and let it out again. This helped.

When she heard Callista again, she was about to tell her to keep trying, but then she heard the words. "We're here."

The sun was going down. Though her eyes had been open, she hadn't noticed. This was the deepest she had gone outside of her room at the back of the bar.

Trilina looked around, and everyone else was down from their horses. They were on the edge of a small stand of trees. She breathed in the evening air and focused on one of the trees. In her mind, she said the words to the push spell. A wave flew out from her and blasted the tree, uprooting it, and causing everyone to turn and stare.

Marl asked, "What happened?"

"Nothing, I was just trying out a spell."

"What sort of spell?"

"It pushes people away."

"Well, it looks like you got it," he said and went back to working on the campfire.

Trilina got down from her horse. She asked Callista and Matilda how it went. They both said it was hard not to have stray thoughts of other things, but they would keep trying.

The question came back to Trilina. *Would she be able*

to get in the state of flow in a battle?

The practice that afternoon had been encouraging. Trilina would do more of it tomorrow. For now, though, she needed to help with the camp duties. She was in charge of the horses and with Rhysdan would check their hooves and take off the saddles. Before bed, the two of them would saddle up the horses again, so if they should need to move quickly in the middle of the night, they'd be ready. But for now, they got a break to graze.

When the day ended, she had a full belly. She hoped to herself that it would be a while before they found the dragon. Every day she got to practice helped.

Still, it had been a good day. And it was nice to have friends along for the journey.

CHAPTER THIRTY-TWO

Marl had them up before the sun. He wanted to make it to Tarnton Baston before mid-day. He had once known some soldiers there and hoped they'd know something about the dragon. One could see the Fog from the baston's tower. If a red dragon had been flying around, they would know it.

From a distance, he could tell that something was up. The last time he'd been to Tarnton, there had been dozens of tents, a building for the blacksmith, and an archery range. What he saw now, was a burned-out shell that must have been the smithy, and black charred land all around.

"Kal and Callista, bows out, arrow nocked, and get behind us. Rhysdan down the right, Elora take up the left. Matilda, you ride behind me and start playing. If the guys in that tower are alive, they'll be pretty edgy. Trilina, I don't know what you do, but get ready to do it. If we see the dragon, hit it in the face with your tree spell."

Trilina nodded.

As they approached, they saw a face appeared at the top of the tower. It looked young and frightened. A voice called out, "Oi, who goes there?"

Marl motioned for Kal and Callista to lower their bows. "I'm Marl Faramound, and I served in the King's army. Who's in charge?"

The face disappeared.

When Marl got to the gate, he stopped. A short while later, a bolt slid with a familiar heavy metal on metal sound, and the smaller door in the guardhouse next to the gate opened up. A stout man with a thick red beard came out with a battle axe resting on his shoulder.

The man squinted. "Is that you, Marl? When did you get so ugly?"

Marl got down off his horse. "When did you get so fat?" he replied and gave his friend a big hug. He turned back to the party and said, "This is Oritas Kutheck, and if you like hearing a good story, none tell it better."

Oritas grinned broadly. "We'll do proper introductions inside, and it's not safe to be milling about out here."

The gate opened, and two ragged looking soldiers waved them in.

One said, "Quickly now, we need to get the horses inside the livery." He ran off to the right where a third man held the door open and urged them inside.

Marl thought it odd that the place was clean and that all the stalls were empty. "Where are your horses?"

Oritas had followed and was standing by the man holding the door. He said something to the soldier, who then ran off. "That story, well, it's one we'll get to once everyone is inside."

The two soldiers returned from the gate with the third that had run off to get them. Ortis told them to get them into the stalls, make sure they had fresh hay and water, and then to get back to the tower. With that, he closed the livery door and motioned for Marl and his friends to follow.

They walked through a side door, which led to a covered walkway to another building, his office. "We'll go over to the mess hall."

Marl asked, "You've built this place up quite a bit since I was last here."

"Aye, it used just to be the tower and the stables. It took about four years, but we added the wall, my office, one barracks for the men stationed here, a mess hall, the armory, and storage house. It started as a way to keep the men busy and in shape. I guess this stonework stuff is in my blood. Dad would have been proud."

"I only met him the once, but you've told me all about his skill with a hammer and chisel," Marl said, as they entered the mess hall. "I see they made you a captain."

Oritas laughed. "Nobody wanted this post. And after they saw what me and the lads were building,

General Massimo himself came out and took a tour. Promoted me on the spot. That was about three years ago," he said and motioned for everyone to grab a seat around the big table in the center of the room.

Marl introduced each member of the party, and Oritas greeted each one like they were a long-lost brother or sister.

When Marl introduced Elora, Oritas asked, "Haven't we met?"

She said, "I'm Marl's sister-in-law, maybe you met his wife?"

Oritas' jovial smile turned down. "Ah, yes, I see it now. That was a tragic loss, her and the wee one," he said, turned back to Marl. "I'm so sorry, my friend."

"Thank you."

Elora sat down, and Marl grabbed a seat next to her.

Oritas grew jovial again. "Okay, I've got a tale of woe, but it will go down better if we had some good coffee. Now, I'm crap at making the brew. Any of you lot any good?"

Matilda raised her hand, almost excited. "I make great coffee."

Callista stood and said, "I'll help Matilda, and we'll have it up in a jiffy."

Oritas sat down. "So, things are dire here at Tarnton, and it all started three weeks ago," he said, his voice dropping a little lower. "Every other day, we send a patrol out. They ride the Fog line alternating between north and south. The lads ride to Thornpost or Najov, depending on the day, stay the night. At both towns, they have a barracks for the lads. We built those, too. A local keeps the place in ship shape and cooks for them. This is what we do, keep an eye on the Fog.

"About three weeks ago, the patrol was heading out from Najov when a strange group of fighters attacked them. Not really bandits, but not really soldiers."

Rhysdan cleared his throat. "They are followers of Aldrei. I was one of them for a while but escaped. It's like they have a magic spell on people. I heard about when they saw your soldiers."

Oritas looked at Rhysdan and said, "Well, they gave our lads a good fight, and had numbers. We lost one man, and the rest had to ride for their lives. Still, the boys got a few licks in. I'm glad you got out. And knowing what they were, makes sense now that you mention it."

Marl said, "Rhysdan is a good man; we're glad to have him."

"Aye, I know that anyone who rides with you is a good man, even them women," Oritas said, giving a nod to Elora. He continued. "The patrol, a dozen men, now down to eleven, made off for the keep. They rode hard until it was clear they were out of danger, then it came."

Trilina said, "What? The dragon."

"The biggest damn dragon I've ever seen. Well, I wasn't on patrol, but we've seen that beast plenty of times since then, and I can tell you it's massive."

Marl interrupted. "What does it call itself?"

"A northern red that goes by the name Aldrei the Conqueror."

"How can he be so big? That's the wyrmling we chased off just six years ago."

"I dunno, but he's much older than that, now."

Marl could sense the hairs on the back of his neck standing up. "This isn't the sort of news I wanted."

"I know, mate, and the story isn't done," he said, and continued, "Aldrei came out of the Fog. Men had gotten off their horses and were walking them for a stretch. The road was a fair bit off from the Fog wall, so they had a little time. They knew they couldn't outrun it, so they spread out to take on the beast. My best man, a fearless soldier, was the first to fall. He never landed a blow. The four archers in the group, the fifth was the one lost to the attack, did their best to move and fire. I'm told that a few arrows landed on its underbelly, but the dragon's scales on the rest of its body shrugged them off like they were wee little bogger flies."

Callista and Matilda came out of the kitchen holding two mugs of coffee in each hand. They handed them out and took their seats.

Oritas continued, "The rest of the battle is mostly lost, as only one man, the archer you saw at the top of the tower, made it back. He had a few details when men fell and such, but from his position, and focusing on firing until he ran out of arrows, he couldn't remember much else. When his last arrow was gone, he drew his sword, but by then there were only three other soldiers left, and he had to try to make it back to let us know what had happened."

Marl shook his head. "You lost a lot of good men. I'm sorry."

"That was almost half of what's stationed here. What came next was worse," he said and took a sip of his coffee. "Oh, lassie, this is how you make coffee."

Matilda blushed. "Thanks."

"Outside the walls, we had a blacksmith shop which I had hoped to one day put a wall around, but just hadn't gotten to it. There were a handful of tents. General Massimo has long-range patrols that travel the length of the Fog, and when they get here, they stay in the tents. That's about once a month. We need more bastons, but until then, well, it doesn't matter. Two days after we lost my men, just after sunrise, the beast flew out of the Fog. It didn't look as big at first. I didn't realize how high up it could fly. I've never seen such powerful wings. And we've seen a few dragons in our day, eh buddy?"

"That we have."

"Everyone got to their posts. We had fourteen men, including myself, left. It didn't attack, just flew in a giant circle for a long while and then dove like a missile. But it didn't strike or breath fire, it just pulled up at the last moment, veered off, and flew back into the Fog. I think it just wanted us to see what it could do. Put that thought in our minds. The next week, at all times of the day or night, it would come out for a look. On the seventh day, it landed next to the tents and burned them to the ground along with the smithy.

"Now, my men's nerves were long past frazzled.

Nobody was sleeping. The shifts were long. Our supplies, only because we lost so many men, were holding out, but it seemed Aldrei was trying to wear us down. I hated to give up a man, but I needed to get out the word. The few times we'd sent pigeons, Aldrei had known and chased the birds down. We were cut off. We had to risk sending out a rider to try to get word to the capital.

"As I feared, the moment he started riding, the dragon flew out and the poor boy was snatched from his mount and carried away. I can still hear his screams."

Marl asked, "Why didn't Aldrei hear us approaching and attack?"

Oritas thought about that for a while. "That's a good question. I dunno, but I wonder if…" he lost his voice to thought.

The room sat still, letting him think.

"My granddad used to tell us about dragons. He had all sorts of stories, and I'd say most of them were heavy on story and light on fact. Granddad had a way of exaggerating, but maybe this one bit was true. There was a dragon he talked about, I don't remember the name, but it was blind. Couldn't see a thing, but would learn the sound of a person's heart, supposedly, and could recognize one person from the next. Now, this dragon wasn't aggressive, and never caused folks any harm, aside from the occasional bit of lost livestock, which it always left a bag of coin on the farmers stoop with more gold than the animal was worth.

"I wish I could remember its name. It doesn't matter, but maybe that's what Aldrei was doing on that first day, learning who we were. Or maybe he's not watching and listening all the time, just most of it."

Marl finished off his coffee. "What happened after Aldrei burned the tents?"

"Well, we get a supply shipment every three weeks. Four soldiers from the capital bring it. We were doing okay since we'd lost half our men. I had everyone on the lookout for the caravan. Arrows nocked and all, as I expected they wouldn't make it to the gate. I prayed I was wrong.

"I wasn't. Maybe it was just bad luck, but when they rounded the bend in the road, Aldrei was circling overhead and spotted them. All four carts headed off in different directions, and he chased each one down. None of them made it to our gate. That sight hit the lads pretty hard.

"Three days ago, I asked for volunteers, seven men, all would take our last seven horses and ride out in different directions. We saw two of them fall but have no idea if any of the others made it. And that's our story, up until you rode up to our gates without being harassed. I'm starting to think you're just damn lucky, Marl."

"This doesn't feel like luck."

The somber faces around the table nodded. Nobody was enjoying the adventure anymore. Marl knew they were way in over their heads.

And then they heard the wings.

CHAPTER THIRTY-THREE

Marl said, "Was that?"

Oritas jumped to his feet. "Well, it looks like you'll get to see the dragon after all. This way," he said and ran out of the mess hall and across to the tower.

It took only seconds to cross the small courtyard. Everyone filed through the door, and Oritas slammed it shut, and climbed the stairs. All four archers manned slits in the tower, bows at the ready. "We don't go up top because there's little point."

Marl pushed his way past and climbed the ladder and said, "Everyone stays here; we're not fighting Aldrei today unless we have no choice, but get your weapons ready."

Oritas followed up the ladder.

Marl said, "I just need to see it, you don't need to…"

"Nonsense, it would be rude of me not to

reintroduce you."

"Have you talked with it?

"Once."

Marl saw the shadow first and then looked to the sky. In long winding arcs, the northern red flew above the keep. Its head was looking down and, as if it was trying to remember, cocked it to one side. Then dove. Marl said, "Get down."

They ducked down.

A wave of air brushed past them as the dragon swooped past. It banked and then landed on the far wall. "It seems you have some guests, Oritas. And I believe one of them is my old friend Marl. Did you think I'd forgotten you?"

Marl stood up. "Why are you back, Aldrei?"

"You chased me out of my home, and I've returned to take what's mine…and for a pound of flesh. Your flesh, to be precise," the dragon said with a hiss. He blew an arc of fire into the air, well over their heads.

"I chased you out once, this time leaving won't be an option. I'll see you dead."

The dragon laughed. "Will you now? You and Oritas, with his mighty axe and his four cowering archers. I was stupid last time—arrogant—and I've got the scars to prove it. I'm older now, much older, and I fight to win. It's you whose days are numbered. This is where you die," he said, gave a flap of his wings, rose up in the air, flew past them and off into the Fog.

Oritas said, "That was some mighty fine bravado,

but do you have a plan to back it up?"

Marl clapped his friend on the back. "Nope, but at least we can get back to that coffee. Matilda does have a gift."

Oritas roared with laughter. "Well, then we best figure out our next move."

Marl descended the ladder first, and the faces of the soldiers and his team told the tale. They were frightened. Marl said, "We've got work to do. Matilda, we're going to need a lot more coffee."

Her voice trembled a little when she said, "I'll make a couple of pots and keep it coming."

CHAPTER THIRTY-FOUR

Marl looked around the table and met each person's eye. He turned to Oritas and said, "This is your post; with your permission, I'd like to lay things out as I see them."

Oritas stood and said, "I've known you for a long time. My men are mostly dead, and the four that remain are broken and exhausted. We've not slept in days. The gods sent you to our door for a reason. You and I have fought enough battles together that I know you've got a good mind for strategy. If you've got a plan, then my men and I will do what we can. We're at your service my friend."

Marl clasped forearms with Oritas, gave him a nod, and said, "This was not what you all signed up for. We headed out to rid this land of the menace of a dragon, Aldrei, but this is not the dragon I expected to find. I can't explain how he could have aged so much, perhaps it's something about that fog, but this is a fully grown, mature beast that thrives on destruction. He was a bastard as a wyrmling. The strength and power are ten times what I thought we'd be facing. It looks dire."

Matilda said, "Are we going to die?"

He could tell it was the question on everyone's mind. Matilda's shoulders slumped, and she wore a look more of resignation than fear. Elora and Kal weren't showing it, but the others were worried, except for Trilina. She sat with a straight back, hands on the table, eyes clear and bright, taking in every word. Marl said, "There have been greater challenges in the history of warfare than what we face in this keep. Battles where heroes have emerged, and the odds were beaten, where strength has been found, and foes are slain. Oritas and I have seen it."

Oritas bobbed his head up and down. "It's true, we've been in some tight spots, but as long as Marl's blade is beside me, I know there's a chance."

Marl went on. "Matilda, this is not the time for false promises. Some may die, or maybe all, but we have weapons Aldrei doesn't know about. We have your lute, Trilina's wand, six archers, and some fine wielders of steel. And we've got a fine witch in Callista, who works miracles with her balms and potions."

Callista said, "I'll heal you up faster than you can imagine."

Marl asked, "Who's been handling the cooking?"

Oritas said, "The lads have been taking turns, but

none of them knows their way around the kitchen. Our cook was killed by the beast coming back with vegetables from a farmer a day's ride from here. He was out when we got the news about the patrol, or I would have never let him go."

The mood was starting to shift, Marl sensed it. He said, "The first thing we need to do is get your men in the tower some rest...and hope. Oritas, with your permission, I'd like Rhysdan to relieve your men and send them down here."

"We're all your men now. Come with me, Rhysdan."

Marl said, "I want you," looking at Matilda, "Kal, and Callista to go find out what they have for food. We need to get his men their strength back. A good meal and some sleep will go a long way."

Kal said, "On it."

When Oritas returned with the four archers, Marl said, "Okay, you've had a rough go. But we're going to get some food in your bellies, and then you're all to get some rest. Do you still have some fight left in you?"

One of them said, "You've brought us hope. We've got a good deal of fight left in us."

Matilda came back out from the kitchen and said, "We're going to whip up a bit of stew. How does that sound?"

Oritas said, "We've mostly been eating jerky, that'll be much appreciated."

Marl asked, "How are you fixed for arrows?"

"The one thing we won't run out of is arrows," Oritas said.

"Anything heavier?"

"We've got three ballistas, but they all need repairs."

Marl said, "Elora is one of the finest woodworkers I know."

Elora stood up. "I'll take a look."

Oritas said, "They've each got some broken bits. If you can craft the parts we need to get them working, I'd be grateful. I'll show you where they're at."

Marl motioned for Trilina to join him. He left the four archers to wait for their food and headed outside. "I've never liked magic, but we're going to need you. And maybe I've been too quick to judge. What sorts of things can you do, besides taking out trees?"

"I've got a spell that summons a huge wolf. One of the spells causes panic, and the person thinks ghosts are attacking them. You saw the push spell, but if I'm truthful, I don't think it was supposed to have that much push."

"Do you think it could have knocked the dragon off the wall?"

Trilina thought for a moment. "I think, given enough practice, I could learn to make it that strong."

Marl thought about this for a while. "That could be helpful. What about that wand?"

"It shoots shards of ice," she said and added, "but I don't know if that would damage the dragon or not."

"I'm sure we'll find out. Any other tricks?"

"There are hundreds of spells that mages can do,

but I don't know them. They get progressively harder the more powerful the spell, and I'm still relatively new. But I might be able to learn one or two more before we need it if it's not too complex. Do you want to see the book?"

"Are there any others like the wolf? Anything with wings?"

"I'll have to look. Until now, I've just been studying the ones I mentioned."

"I've just got one more question."

Trilina waited.

"Matilda may have more power than just that lute. Elora thinks she might be able to cast spells. Do you think you could teach her any of the spells?"

"While we were riding, both she and Callista wanted me to teach them. I'll try, and I'll start with the wolf spell."

"Good thinking. Now, grab your stuff from the saddlebags and ask Oritas if there is a quiet place you can use. You may be the key."

Trilina gave a confident smile. "I've got magic in me. I'll get the girls up to speed."

"I know you will," he said and watched as she ran to the stables to get her gear.

The courtyard was small. It looked just big enough that Aldrei could land there. *But how could they make that happen?* he thought. Of all the possible scenarios, getting the dragon into the confined space would give them the best chance. Aldrei had cut off the keep from supplies, and he was trying to starve them out. That showed the dragon was a tactician. It made Marl wonder about the beast's end game.

This was going to be hard, but his first step was done.

Everyone was on board.

CHAPTER THIRTY-FIVE

Marl stood at the door next to the mess hall. He looked up at the tower, and the archer who was keeping an eye on things gave a nod and smiled. Oritas' men had bounced back nicely once they got some rest.

Matilda crossed the courtyard and asked, "Could I get you a cup of coffee?"

"I'm fine, thanks."

"Do you mind if I have one and we talk?" she asked.

Marl opened the door and held it for her.

As she went off to put the coffee on, Marl thought about the state of things.

It had been three days, and they were getting into a routine. The dragon showed three or four times each day, mostly just circled, but occasionally sprayed fire down on the keep. Anything that could be burned, though, had been, so it did little additional damage.

Matilda returned. "It will be a little bit. I decided to go with tea instead."

"Well, I might have a cup of tea, now that you mention it."

She smiled. "Oh, there will be plenty."

"What did you want to talk about?"

She looked at him, then spread out her skirt and looked away. For a moment it looked like she was about to say something and then stopped.

"It's okay; you can tell me what's on your mind."

"It's my parents. I know we have a lot going on. And we're trapped here. I can't stop thinking about them. Trilina has been trying to teach Callista and me how to quiet our minds..." her voice faded to silence.

"How is that going?"

"Callista is doing well, but I can't stop thinking about Mom and Dad. I don't know if they're okay. And do you know what bothers me the most, the one thing that I can't get out of my head?"

"What's that?"

"What if I don't make it? What if the dragon eats me up or burns me to a crisp?"

"Death can be frightening when one looks it in the face. I'm sure that everyone here feels it."

"Oh, no, it's not that, it's how will they know what happened to me? If one day they're okay and I'm just gone. I can't stand that thought. My mom, she worries a lot. It would be worse for her not to know than to know.'"

Marl said, "I promise that if something happens

to you, I'll find them and let them know how you helped us fight."

"But what if something happens to you, too?"

"Well, I'll tell all the others to do the same."

Matilda looked at him and then shrugged a little.

Marl added, "And if we should all perish, is that what you're wondering?"

A sheepish "Yes," was all she said.

Marl understood. "I have an idea, what if we write a letter to her and hide it with something of yours here in the keep. Then, when Aldrei's worshipers search they'll find it."

"But how do I know my parents will ever see it?"

"Because at the end of the letter, we write something in that only your parents will know, that looks like code and hint that it is something more valuable than gold or jewels, we hint that you've found a powerful amulet. This will make whoever finds it, go and talk to them. And they will read your letter."

Matilda's eyes got wet, and a tear rolled down her face. "That will be perfect." She hugged him and jumped to her feet. "I'm going to make you the best cup of tea you've ever had. And then I'm going to go back and try quieting my mind some more."

Oritas passed Matilda as she dashed off into the kitchen. He sat down across from Marl and said, "How about we play a game of chess?"

"I haven't played in years. Such an odd game, and that fellow who taught us, he was so strange, both foreign and familiar. But if you've still got the board…"

"I keep it over here. All the lads play now, and we've made a few more sets. It's great for focus," he said and went to a chest in the corner.

They set up the pieces and began.

This is how they had spent their evenings when they were in their twenties. The time between battles was mostly training and complaining, and this strange game was a great distraction.

Oritas moved his pawn and said, "You've got my boys back in fine spirits. I'm feeling better, too. Have you got a plan for how we can bring down that beast?"

Marl moved his knight to attack the pawn and said, "How's Elora doing with the ballistas?"

"She's got one of them good as new. I think she's close on the second. They were in pretty bad shape. I should have had my men working on them months ago."

"I thought we could hide them in the courtyard and try to get Aldrei to land. At point blank, I'm sure they'd go through his belly, and with three different placements, we're sure to get a shot."

"That's brilliant, but how do we coax him to land?"

"I haven't worked that bit out yet. We need to make Aldrei mad. He's smart and will see the tactical advantage we have in the courtyard, so I don't know if we can pull it off."

"How does one piss off a dragon?"

"What do we know about their sleep? Do you remember anything from our training?"

"Oi, that was a long time ago. I remember that each breed is different, but they all have to sleep some. And that dragons are light sleepers, keep listening, so it's hard to sneak up on them, nigh on impossible."

"Are you going to move?" Marl asked

Oritas reinforced his pawn with another pawn.

Marl considered this for a bit and moved his bishop to support the knight. "I wasn't thinking of trying to sneak up on Aldrei, and I was wondering if we could wear him out?"

"How?"

"What happened whenever someone tried to leave or approach?"

"Well, except for you, the dragon appeared and chased them down."

"How far did they get before he caught the first man?"

"He made it maybe half a kilometer down the road, riding like the wind," Oritas said as he brought another knight into the game.

Matilda returned with two cups of tea. "I thought you might like a cup, too."

"I would indeed, lassie. Thanks," Oritas said looking up from the board.

Marl wasn't focused on the board. He said, "If the first man was on your fastest horse..."

"He was."

"Then at top speed, over an hour, he could travel forty eight kilometers, give or take."

"Aye, but no horse can run top speed for that long."

"I know, but in the first half kilometer that's how fast he would have been going."

"True."

"That's eight tenths of a kilometer in a minute, or..." And Marl thought for a bit. "Point zero one three per second. So, if he was going flat out, he was caught at about the thirty-seven-second mark, though let's say it was thirty five, to account for getting up to speed."

Oritas took a sip of his tea. "What are you thinking?"

"If the dragon is just on the other side of the Fog line, he must be watching or listening all the time to react so quickly."

"Sure, but how does that help us? And Aldrei wasn't that quick when you arrived."

"That's a good point; maybe he was away?"

"He has to eat sometime," Oritas said.

"That's true," Marl said. "Have you seen him hunting?"

"No, so he must be doing that elsewhere."

Marl stood up. "Let me think." He started to pace while his friend went back to staring at the board. In his mind, he was trying to see all the possible moves Aldrei could make. And no matter what, he needed to sleep and eat. That could be their window of opportunity. Marl sat back down and said, "Okay, if we could get word to General Massimo, we'd only need to hunker down and survive."

"Yes, but we've tried that," Oritas said.

"It's a double attack."

"What is?"

Marl slid all the pieces off the board and set up a rook near one edge. "This edge is the Fog. The rook is the keep."

"Okay."

Marl set a knight three squares from the rook and said, "This is just under a quarter kilometer. We ride out to this spot, and the moment the dragon appears, we turn and ride back to the safety of the keep."

"The time from when the dragon appears, usually in a power dive, to the moment he killed the first rider wasn't as much as the time from when the rider left to when we first saw it."

"He must be further in the Fog, or it takes a bit for him to realize. That's a good point, so instead, we ride out to no more than a quarter kilometer, spin and start back. He'll already be heading our way by that point."

"I agree, but what does that get us?"

"Hopefully, fatigue."

"You lost me, old friend."

"If he intends to keep us from getting the word out, and we keep feigning a rider making a break for it, throughout the day, when will he eat or rest? And eventually, he may be too worn out to chase, that will be when the rider doesn't stop."

"How will the rider know when he's not going to chase?"

"If he makes it back and Aldrei doesn't appear, then we send him out again. If he gets to the quarter kilometer mark, and we still don't see him, he keeps going."

Oritas leaned back. "That's why you always beat me in chess. You see the future better than I do. And I know I get pretty grumpy when I've missed a meal," he said patting his belly.

"When have you ever missed a meal?"

"Let's set the board back up and finish this game. Then we will figure out a schedule to start messing with Aldrei."

CHAPTER THIRTY-SIX

Marl considered the food supply. It was running low. It had been fine for five people, but now they were twelve, and there hadn't been a resupply; they had been there a week. Elora had all three ballistas fixed. Two were hidden behind crates, and one was set back in the stables, far enough that it couldn't be seen.

There weren't any more days to prepare. For better or worse, he had to start his plan now. The only question was, how long would it take to piss off or wear down Aldrei?

Callista had lobbied hard to be the first rider, but Marl said they couldn't risk her and her healing skills. Kal had volunteered next, but that wouldn't work either, they needed his bow on the tower.

In the end, Marl knew that he was the only volunteer that made sense. The details of his plan had been drilled into everyone's head. Oritas was back in charge and would manage the attack if they succeeded in drawing Aldrei into the courtyard.

With each person at their post, Marl said to Elora as he sat astride his horse. "You know I think about them every day."

"They loved you more than you could know. And my sister wouldn't want you getting eaten by a dragon, so you do your sprint and get back here, Marl."

They opened the gate, and he was off.

Marl had done a bit more math, and he was thinking about it as he rode. A bolt fired from one of the ballistas out to its maximum range, set the boundary at five hundred meters. Then they had fired another at half that distance. It was this second bolt that was his target.

He wasn't wearing any armor, as that was more weight on the horse. If his assumptions about the dragon had been wrong, well, a little extra protection wasn't going to save him.

Matilda was on the tower with the archers. The moment she saw the dragon come out of the Fog, she would blow a horn she'd found among one of the dead soldier's belongings.

The horse thundered under him, and the wind blew past his ears. His eyes focused on that bolt poking out of the ground. He had to reach and make the turn well before the horn blew or he wouldn't make it back. Each second seemed to slow. The edges of the world faded. He was almost there.

Marl edged the horse out a bit and readied for the turn. Nothing from the tower.

He reached the bolt, a six-foot javelin with brass feathering and painted red, to make it easier to see. The horse turned like a champ, and they were headed back to safety.

Now Marl could see the Fog wall that lay only nine hundred meters behind the keep. And there was Aldrei, darting out of the Fog. In his wake, a swirl of cloud pulled from the wall and trailed after the dragon. Two powerful flaps of his wings, and he began his dive.

He dug his heels into the horse and asked for more. The horse gave it all he had. They could both see the dragon.

It was going to be close.

Each second, they closed the gap to the gate.

Marl could see the eyes of Aldrei glaring at him. He imagined the hate the beast must feel. And he rode on.

He was almost there, and so was Aldrei, who would pass straight over the bastion. Just a few more seconds.

A volley of arrows flew up at the dragon as it got near. Two stuck in its chest, but Aldrei didn't stop his dive.

At the last moment, the giant northern red spread its wings and spun back toward the gate, breathing a stream of fire, just as Marl passed through, and the ironwork came crashing down. He and the horse were spared by only a few meters.

The archers kept firing, but they did little damage. The giant beast flapped his wings, took to the air, laughing. "You'll not get away that easily you coward. Running away and leaving your friends. I should have known."

Marl signaled, and the archers left for the safety of the tower, while Marl got the horse back to the livery. Elora closed the door behind him and said, "You ride pretty good for an old man."

"Thanks. Now, let's get ready for round two in an hour."

CHAPTER THIRTY-SEVEN

Marl sat down across from Oritas and said, "Two days of this has been harder than I imagined."

"Yes, but his reaction time seems to be slowing. And switching riders and directions they bolt from the keep was a good idea."

"The food is nearly gone. Even if Aldrei stops chasing us, and we could get a rider away, we might all be dead from starvation," Marl said, sipping a coffee.

Oritas looked resigned to what fate had to offer. "We will fight to the end; you've given us a chance my friend. We better get out there."

Marl stood and followed his friend out of the mess.

The fog wall, as it did every morning at sunrise, seemed to glow.

By the gate, Elora sat astride her horse, its breath curling from its nose, as its hooves stomped. Her mount had always loved to run, and it seemed it was ready. "I've heard your speech to every other rider, let's skip it and open the gate. I'll be back in thirty seconds. And yes, I'll be careful."

Marl said, "Don't fall off."

Her head snapped around, and she said, "That was one time, after your wedding reception, and I was drunk. When will you let it go?"

"Next week, when we're back at my inn, celebrating."

For all her hardness, Marl knew how to take Elora's edge off. "I'll buy the first round," she said, the gate opened, and then with a "Ha," and a sharp kick, they were off.

Marl watched from the open gate, the dust flying up behind her. He didn't know anyone who rode as well as Elora.

Oritas said, "She's better than you on a horse."

"I know," Marl said, with a little bit of family pride. He looked up to the tower. Matilda, rubbing the sleep out of her eyes, gave the hand signal that she was watching the Fog wall, and it was clear.

Their plan to keep Aldrei from eating or sleeping had taken its toll on them, too. In between rides, each of them tried to work in cat naps, but it wasn't the same as getting a full night's rest.

Elora was about to make the turn when he saw it —pouring out from the trees at the bend in the road, about one kilometer from the keep, people with weapons.

Marl drew his sword out of instinct.

Oritas already had his axe at the ready.

Elora slid to a stop.

It wasn't just the people, but behind them, glistening in the glow of the early morning light, the red scales of Aldrei. He took to the air.

Marl yelled, "Archers ready, facing front."

Elora spun and headed back.

Aldrei closed on her.

Marl screamed, running toward her approaching horse, "Faster."

The mob of people was running toward them, too, though they were still a ways off.

Elora slapped her reins back and forth across the neck of her horse, and she was giving all she had.

The dragon was faster.

It flew through the first barrage of arrows, like they were nothing, and let out a massive stream of flames that swept across Elora. She screamed. The horse fell. Her body flung forward.

Marl and Oritas closed the gap and came to a stop just on the other side of Elora, as the dragon unfurled its wings and landed.

Aldrei said, "I've waited for this day. I've dreamt of each night. And now, it is your turn to suffer. Your death will be slow."

Marl and Oritas ran forward and attacked.

They each landed blows that cut deep.

Aldrei swiped at Oritas and batted him away, sending him flying through the air. He landed with a clatter of armor.

Marl ducked under Aldrei's attempt to bite him, he

thrust up toward the beast's neck, but the blow didn't land. Marl spun and landed a massive blow to the dragon's side. Its heavier scales absorbed the damage.

He heard another round of arrows whizzing past. The dragon tried to knock Marl down with a swipe of his claws, but Marl dove out of the way.

The beast reared up.

Marl didn't have time to get to his feet.

Aldrei screamed, "Die!"

Time seemed to slow. Marl became acutely aware of everything around him. *Is this the moment before death?* He thought. Three arrows flew over him in rapid succession and then a fourth. Their flight path was too low.

He heard running steps, and it had to be Kal and one of the other archers. Only Kal could get off three shots so fast. All the arrows landed in the belly of Aldrei, and it stunned him for a moment.

A wolf, then another, leaped over him and went for each of the dragon's legs.

Marl scrambled to his feet.

Oritas, face bloodied, axe in hand, ran from Marl's right and landed a massive blow to the side of the beast.

Aldrei brought his tail around and knocked Oritas off his feet.

Marl, thrust his sword to the chest of the dragon, but Aldrei, in one move, with a wolf dug into its left leg, parried the blow and flung the wolf aside.

The dragon pushed off and took flight just as another four arrows landed in its chest. It flew up, banked, and sent another wave of fire to the ground. The two wolves and Oritas were caught in its path— Marl dove out of the way at the last moment.

The mob was gaining on them.

There was a hundred meters between them and the keep. Elora was in bad shape. Oritas wasn't moving. Marl grabbed his sister-in-law and slung her over his shoulder, just as Kal and Callista got to him. "Get back to the keep."

Then he saw it, Oritas' hand moved. He wasn't dead. Marl turned to Kal, "Here, take Elora."

"Callista, come with me."

Marl sprinted to his friend. "We've got you."

Callista said something that Marl didn't understand.

Oritas' eyes opened. He looked dazed.

Callista dropped her bow, knelt beside him and poured a potion down Oritas' throat. "I need you to try to get up."

Marl saw his eyes clear and helped him to his feet.

Callista picked up her bow.

It was a mob of a few hundred, some with armor and swords, others with just clubs and spears. They were almost on them.

"Run," Marl commanded.

They turned toward the keep and saw it, Aldrei in front of the gate, Kal and Elora lying off to the side. Another wolf had been summoned, and it was distracting the dragon.

Marl said as they ran, "Callista, see if you can help them."

Callista slung her bow over her shoulder and ran towards Kal and Elora.

Arrows from the tower flew overhead toward the approaching mob. Marl couldn't see them, but the sounds of their running were clear. They were about to be caught between a dragon and a crowd.

Aldrei grabbed the wolf in its jaws and bit down. The beast went limp. With a flick of its head, the dragon tossed the body at them, and almost hit Oritas. Marl lunged and landed a blow on the dragon's right leg.

Oritas swung a huge arcing blow to the other leg.

Marl heard a loud wooden twang and knew that someone had just fired one of the ballistas. From Aldrei's scream, he knew it had landed. Aldrei took to the sky again, but as he did, he caught Marl with his tail and knocked him to the ground.

The mob was nearly on them.

Oritas swung his axe in a circle, and it kept them back long enough for Marl to get to his feet.

Behind them, dozens of people were rushing to Callista's position, but Marl couldn't see them through the crowd.

He positioned himself back to back with Oritas, and they fought. Their foe was untrained but had numbers. A spear dug into Marl's side. He heard a blow from a club land on Oritas. Still, they fought.

Marl drove his sword through a young man's chest. His look went from dull and mindless, to alert, then confused, and he dropped. An older man, with a pitchfork, thrust it at Marl's chest. He blocked with his sword, lifted, and tore the weapon from the man's hands and then brought the sword down splitting the man's skull.

A woman, with a sword, who didn't seem like she knew how to use it, raised the weapon over her head, but then fell at Marl's feet. He saw Trilina coming through the gate with Rhysdan by her side. She held her wand and looked calm, like a veteran warrior. Another wolf appeared and bound off in the direction of Callista, Kal, and Elora.

Marl could hear the wings of the dragon as it circled overhead. Then he heard something else, the lute, and Matilda's voice ringing out.

The mob slowed.

Marl lunged forward waving his sword. Oritas stayed at his back. The mob, no longer swinging their weapons parted. He moved toward where he'd seen Callista run.

On the ground, lying next to Kal, with a potion in her hand and a nasty head wound, she looked dead. Elora, still burned, but looking better had her eyes open but wasn't moving. Maybe Callista had gotten a potion down her throat before she was hit.

Rhysdan took up a position next to Marl, and Trilina fell in on the other side, wand at the ready. The mob continued to disperse. Marl said, "We need to get them inside. Trilina, see if you can get that potion into Callista."

The horses hooves thundered over Matilda's playing. As the people slowly came out of their trance, they seemed confused and disoriented. Marl could see it was Cauldor and flanked on both sides were a dozen men in full plate armor. They had been watching the battle from outside the range of the tower archer, but now they were bearing down on them.

Then there was silence, followed by a scream.

Marl looked up, and Aldrei was on the tower. Matilda's music was gone. An archer was tossed from the tower and landed three meters from them, then another, and the blood-curdling scream of the third. Marl expected to see one more, but maybe he had gotten to safety.

The wings spread and up flew Aldrei, Matilda clutched in his talons, screaming.

Rhysdan yelled, "Matilda! Noooo."

The horses closed.

An explosion just in front of the party filled the air with a roiling black cloud as dark as night. Marl had seen that cloud before. He grabbed Oritas by the arm and said, "Grab Callista, and follow me." Marl threw his sword through the cloud, bent down, pulled Elora up onto his shoulders and said, "Rhysdan and Trilina, pick up Kal." He ran through the cloud and came out the other side, just like before, standing in a vast desert.

Marl collapsed to the ground by his sword, and Elora rolled off his shoulder next to him. Oritas made it through, followed by Rhysdan and Trilina with Kal by the arms and legs.

The cloud faded and, in its place, a man in a suit and bowler hat. He looked nothing like the jovial fellow who had given them the poisoned tea.

Marl, gasping for breath, asked, "Who are you?"

"I go by many names, and magic lets me change my face. There is someone who would like to meet you."

Rhysdan gasped, "What about Matilda? We need to go back!"

The man shook his head. "She's with the dragon now, in the Fog. That battle is lost. Let's get everyone a little healthier before we head out. We've got a long journey ahead."

CHAPTER THIRTY-EIGHT

Marl got to his feet. "If you won't tell me your name, at least explain why you saved us when the first time we met, you tried to poison Callista and me."

The man tilted his head to one side and then the other. "That's fair, I should explain. I wasn't trying to poison you, not in the least. What Callista drank, in the tea, was a weak magical charm that gives one strength and leaves a trace that the monks can see. It was the same for that one," he said, pointing to Kal, who was lying with his eyes open but not moving. "Something is coming, and the world you live in, the cozy existence mostly free of war, is about change."

Marl said, "Mostly free of war. I've fought many battles. I'd hardly say it was a 'cozy existence.'"

"When you look back, should you survive, you'll remember this moment and realize that war has many shades, and it's about to get midnight black."

Kal lifted his head. "Not to interrupt. Still not feeling so great over here. Any chance you have some of that tea that gives you strength? I'll take a double."

Marl picked his sword off the sand and returned it to its sheath. He looked at the man, then looked down at Elora, who was trying to sit up and was shaking all over. "The burning, it hurts." Marl sat down next to her and wrapped his arms around her shoulders.

Oritas was holding Callista and trying to get her to wake up. He asked the man, "Can you heal her?"

"Yes, and I do suppose you should have some name to call me; let's go with Maltese Gato."

Oritas said, "Well, Maltese, get to it then. She's barely breathing."

Marl watched, as did the others, and the strange little man in his odd suit and hat leaned over and laid his hands on the gash at the back of her head. His thin face relaxed, eyes closed, and with barely a whisper began to chant. A faint yellow light grew out from where he touched Callista.

Her head shot up, and she screamed, "Hang in there, Kal, I've got..."

Maltese stepped back and said, "You're okay, the battle is over. You lost but survived."

"Where are we?"

Oritas said, "No idea, lassie, but this is the man we need to thank."

Marl said, "You'll need to rest, but do you have any of that balm left? Elora's in bad shape."

Callista tried to get up, but her legs weren't ready. "Yes, I've got all my supplies laid out next to them," she paused and looked around.

Maltese knelt next to Elora. "I know our first meeting didn't go so great back at the little house in the woods…"

Still shaking in Marl's arms, she said, "You were the old woman we helped from the ditch?"

"That's how I appeared, yes."

Maltese pulled a small vial from his vest pocket. "This will help with the pain if you'll trust me."

"I don't trust you, but I'll take it," she said holding out a shaky hand.

Marl took the vial, opened it, and said, "Open up."

Elora did as she was told.

The trembling slowed.

Maltese said, "I can heal you, too, but it will take a little time." He pulled a second vial out of his vest and motioned for Rhysdan to hand it to Kal. "This will help you, while I work on your friend."

Kal said, "Thanks. And for the record, I liked the tea."

"Lay her down, and I'll get to work," Maltese said.

Trilina asked, "Is there anything I can do?"

Looking up from Elora, Maltese stared at her for a long time. "There is much you can do, but not right now. It's an honor to meet you, the first daughter."

CHAPTER THIRTY-NINE

Marl frowned as he saw Trilina's mouth fall open. Whatever Maltese meant by calling her First Daughter, it was as new to her as to the rest of them. He filed the thought away for later. Seeing his friends healed was far more important to him than titles and vague secrets.

It was apparent that Marl's concern was unfounded. Maltese focused on Elora, chanting as he had before. Bit by bit, the burns faded from her skin, and her face relaxed. Towards the end, the process slowed, Maltese sweating under the hot sun long before he was done.

"We need to create a bit o' shelter," Rhysdan said, looking to Marl.

"Aye, that we do," Oritas replied. "We'll all be a crisp long afore our healer here has done his work."

Once more Marl frowned. They hadn't exactly

brought any of their usual traveling packs with them. They'd all rushed out into the heat of battle.

"There's a tent in my pack," Elora said, her voice easier than it had been since arriving. "Spread the canvas out."

Marl could have hit himself. Of course, she'd ridden out hoping to escape. She'd had a pack on her back ready to travel. It had taken some of the brunt of Aldrei's fire breath but had been extinguished when Elora had been flung from her horse and rolled in the dirt.

Callista used her nimble fingers to pull open the leather backpack. The contents had fared a little better, but the smell of charred animal skin almost made Marl gag.

The tent canvas was mostly intact, one side sporting a few black spots and holes, but they were soon spreading it above the group and looking for props to support the four corners.

The shade provided relief from the fierce sun, and the group huddled underneath, surrounding Maltese as he worked on Elora.

By the time he finished, Kal had sat up; whatever was in the vial Maltese had given him had done its job.

"I may need to rest a few minutes before I tackle your healing as well," the strange fellow said, looking at Kal.

"I'm already feeling a good sight better. I'd still appreciate some of that tea, however."

Maltese smiled. "Of course. It's grown in a small courtyard of a monastery. If you'll all follow me, I'll lead you there shortly."

"Well, if that tea grows there, I'm sold." Kal tried to return the grin Maltese gave him, but it soon turned into a grimace of pain.

"I don't mean to rush you along, but this sun isn't going to get any less fierce or us any less thirsty while we wait for you to help Kal." Marl knew he was giving the stranger a hard time, but he didn't trust him and wanted to get back to fighting Aldrei and rescuing Matilda as soon as possible. He didn't want to think about what might have happened to the young lass. She'd trusted him and Elora. He hoped she was still alive.

Maltese only rested a few more minutes before getting to his feet again and moving over to Kal. For the third time, the strange man placed his hands and started chanting.

The words were as different as the man was, but they had a gentle sort of cadence to them that made Marl feel calmer than he had in days.

The effect wasn't just for his benefit either. Everyone sat or stood, waiting with patience.

They'd been standing in the desert for over an hour by the time Maltese had finished the healing process.

"I'm sorry. That took longer than I'd have hoped. Aldrei's power has grown far beyond the skill of most to counter."

"Yes. About that dragon," Marl said. "We would like to get back to fighting with him. And finding Matilda."

"Of course. I understand." Maltese reached for his bag again and pulled out a simple compass. "If you'll follow me, I will take you to the monastery and introduce you to someone who would very much like to help."

"Follow you? Through this desert?" Oritas planted his feet. "How about we just use that cloud portal trick you've got?"

"Oh, I'm sorry. That must seem frustrating for you. I can't. The monastery doesn't allow it. We'll have to walk. I'm afraid."

"Walk?" Callista helped Elora to her feet and stared out at the hot sand from their small shaded refuge.

"Yes. It's not far." Maltese smiled and consulted his compass. "This way."

Without another word, the strange man walked off. They had no choice but to follow, or be lost in an unknown desert without him as their guide.

His idea of not far didn't match theirs.

Several hours later everyone was pouring with sweat, stumbling through the dunes under the hot sun. More than one of them had tried to fashion some kind of hat out of spare shirts, their armor stripped off and carried under arms or in makeshift slings.

Marl's legs ached from walking in terrain that shifted, and he squinted against the glare of the sun. Several times he'd considered asking their guide just what was going on, but he wasn't sure he trusted his parched mouth and aching throat to deliver his message. Instead, he kept plodding along, hoping the top of the next dune would reveal something other than more sand.

But it didn't. And neither did the next.

As they came to the crest of an unusually large dune, Kal stopped right in front of him, staring ahead. Instead of giving his friend a shove out of the way, Marl followed his gaze. There on the other side of the desert was a red sandstone cliff.

"There. Told you it wasn't far," their bowler-hatted guide said, the grin on his face both genuine and oblivious to their discomfort. He appeared to be as sweaty as they were but otherwise did not indicate that he'd found their journey arduous in the slightest.

It only made Marl feel even more indignant. They couldn't see anything but a cliff. Whatever there was, it wasn't close enough to be seen.

Despite that, the cliff provided a visible target. The party found a last reserve of strength and hurried down to the foot of the red rock face.

Up close, a path could be seen, hollowed out of the rock itself. The entrance to the path was flanked by two stone statues carved from the cliff face: one male, one female, and both smiling, their arms outstretched in a sort of welcome. Marl could have sworn the path hadn't been there a moment earlier, but Maltese approached it like it was familiar.

The party walked single file in a gully so narrow a horse would have struggled to fit without rubbing against both sides. Rhysdan gave Marl a brief nod, hanging back to guard their rear and letting him follow Maltese.

As Marl passed between the two statues, his ears popped, and his skin tingled for a second. And then he was past them. Maltese hurried ahead.

Once inside the gully, Marl couldn't see farther than a few feet. They were forced to follow on, still being led like the blind. It didn't make Marl feel happy trusting their guide, but he knew that they had no choice. This was still preferable to being eaten by a dragon.

They climbed for what felt like ages until, rounding a corner to the left, they came to a window set into the right wall. It showed the most magnificent monastery, carved into the ground beside them out of the stone.

"Wow," Oritas said, his jaw hanging open. "My old pa would have given his right arm to see a building like this."

Maltese grinned. "It is something, isn't it? The monks carved downward. It's one big piece of stone."

"It must have taken years."

"Many. And this is the only way inside. This refuge is a very heavily guarded secret. Not just anyone can find the way in or approach."

Marl raised his eyebrows. Had Maltese just hinted that those statues had been guards of some kind? It might explain why he'd felt so funny passing between them, but Maltese didn't give them any more time to marvel or ask questions.

Springing into action as if he was fresh from a full night's rest, their guide continued. The path now wound downward, curving ever so slightly to the right as the gully grew deeper and darker.

Marl lost track of how many times they must have wound round in circles, the walls growing up above them, and the monastery to the center growing slowly more visible as the air became cooler.

Before long, Marl could make out the sound of running water, but they wound around the monastery yet another time before he spotted the source. Appearing in a channel carved into the left wall was a small stream of water. It gurgled along beside the path as it continued deeper into the monastery-filled hole.

Maltese carried on walking until he realized all of them had stopped to scoop up handfuls of the cold water as it rushed by.

"Oh, yes. Drink as much as you need," he said as if he'd just remembered they were human and capable of drinking. It was unnecessary, however. They were already guzzling.

When Marl's thirst was quenched, he scooped up one last handful. The water had the sweetest, softest taste he'd ever known. It was cold enough that it took the heat of the desert away, but not so cold it lanced pain through the mind.

Not long after he'd finished drinking, the others stopped as well, each one sighing or smiling in contentment.

Maltese waited just long enough for all of them to finish before he beckoned them onward again.

After the refreshing break, Marl found he could think more clearly. He was also pretty sure he noticed Maltese had an extra spring in his step and eagerness about him as he urged them to continue down the path.

Not much further down, the gully took a sharp right-hand turn, and then they stood in a small courtyard in front of the monastery.

From below, the building looked even more impressive than it had from above. Despite being so far down, the stone had been carved and mirrors had been placed in just the right way that the front was lit up by bright sunlight.

"I do so love arriving at this time of day," Maltese said, lingering in front. Marl wondered what he meant for a couple of seconds before he noticed the building was slowly changing color.

"The sun must be setting," Trilina said, "And far quicker than it does in our country."

"Yes," Maltese said, giving no further explanation. The strange man didn't take his eyes off the building as the sunset played out across its face.

Darkness descended after, taking the color out of the scene and hiding both them and the monastery from view. Marl thought he saw several people in robes. Some on each floor. They carried candles and lit others in strategic locations along the way until the front was lit up in an entirely new way.

"I don't think I've ever seen anything so simple and yet so beautiful," Callista said. Maltese beamed at her.

"This way, this way. Someone will be very eager to meet you. Oh yes, they will." Their guide hurried through the only door, beckoning them over his shoulder as he did.

For a moment Marl hesitated, but Kal shrugged and followed Maltese inside. When the others also walked after, Marl was left with little choice but to join them.

The rooms weren't large, but they were as expertly carved as the rest of the building, ornate patterns worked into the ceilings and walls.

Here and there more people in robes bustled along. A few looked their way and whispered among themselves, but most acted oblivious to the new arrivals.

Maltese led them up several flights of stairs to a larger room. It was off the side of a small courtyard built high enough to get the sun during the day.

"Please wait here and rest. I need to find Petran. He's been looking forward to meeting the First Daughter and her friends for a long time."

Before Marl could ask what he meant by his words Maltese scuttled away, closing a wooden door behind him.

"This must be where they grow that tea!" Kal exclaimed, already exploring. Callista had followed him out to the courtyard, and after giving the plant growing there a sniff, she grinned and nodded.

Kal pulled out a knife to take a cutting, but Trilina grabbed his wrist and stopped him.

"I don't think that's a good idea," she said. "What if they notice? We don't know very much about them. It might be sacred."

"Oh, I assure you, it's not," a voice said from the

doorway. "Shall I have one of the brothers fetch you a seed packet?"

Marl whirled around to see a thin man wearing the same robes as most of the rest of the monastery, with one exception. A gold band was sewn around the hood and hem, and a golden rope tied the robe in place around his waist instead of the matching brown the others wore.

A small black goatee hid what Marl suspected would have been a weak chin, and his hood hid graying black hair.

"Could I have one as well?" Callista asked, her eyes lighting up. Marl shook his head, but their new visitor smiled and nodded.

"The tea leaves aside, and we'd like to get back to fighting Aldrei and rescuing Matilda." Marl stepped forward, getting the monk's attention.

"Yes. I can understand your concern. However, I must suggest you stay here for now. You see, Aldrei is just the beginning."

"No, I don't see. We've no reason to trust you lot."

The monk shifted from one foot to the other.

"I'm sorry. This isn't quite how I envisioned our first meeting going. I've been following your actions for some time, Marl. And the rest of you, Kal, Callista, Rhysdan, Elora, Oritas and, of course, Trilina. I'm Petran."

"Well a name's a start, but I still don't know why we should trust you."

The monk frowned and tilted his head to one side, lost in thought. When he righted it again, he looked directly at Marl. Out of a pocket somewhere inside his robe, he pulled a wooden charm affixed on a necklace. Elora gasped while he just stared. It was one from his wedding.

"Where did you get that?"

"A mutual friend. He gave it to me. Said I'd need it one day to prove I could be trusted. I assume it's yours then?"

"You don't know what it is?" Marl asked, taking it back.

"No. As I said, I was just told to keep it till needed. Must admit I had forgotten it was there."

Marl raised his eyebrows but gave the monk a nod. These had only been given to people he and his wife trusted. It was a good start.

"So why are we here?"

"I've been studying Aldrei for some time. You might say that dragons are a bit of a hobby of mine. I lost track of Aldrei not long after you sent him packing six years ago. He only recently returned, and as you are no doubt well aware by now, he's significantly older and larger than he should be."

"Which is why we need to get back and come up with a new plan," Oritas said.

"Of course. I have every desire to send you back, but you're going to need a few items. Artifacts. That sort of thing."

"Artifacts?" Kal asked, his eyes widening. It was obvious he was already sold on whatever Petran was about to suggest.

"Yes. There are several. Each with their own

magical significance. They'll help you defeat Aldrei and get to the bottom of his mysterious aging."

"Then we'd best get started. Matilda might not have that long."

"Ah, yes. About her. I have it on good authority that you'll see her again. She's going to be quite the resourceful young lady."

"I'm still not the sitting around waiting type." Marl didn't hide his impatience. This monk was taking a long time to get to the point. Under the gaze of the group, he shifted a little, evidently uncomfortable with being rushed.

"I'm going to have to ask you try to be patient."

"Why?" Marl asked the word through gritted teeth, his fists clenching.

"Because I don't know exactly where and what all the artifacts are yet. I know you're going to need them. Until then, you need to stay here. It's too dangerous for them—for all of you—to go back without these items."

There was a stunned silence.

"You'd better start finding out what we need," Rhysdan said, "Because we leave in two days regardless. Understood?"

Petran nodded and gulped.

"Perfect," he replied. "In the meantime, please make yourselves comfortable. I'll have the rest of the monks bring you food. And arrange baths."

"You saying we all smell?" Kal asked, grinning through his indignant tone.

"Well, now that you ask." Petran smiled. "The

room does have a certain aroma."

Kal chuckled, and several of the others followed suit. It broke the tension, and Petran slipped away.

Letting out a frustrated sigh, Marl shook his head.

"Easy there, big fella," Oritas said. "We'll go get what we need to rescue your lassie in no time. But we need to rest, heal up, and gather ourselves. If these monks feel inclined to help us, then I reckon we ought to let them."

His friends' words helped soothe him. As long as Matilda could wait then so could he.

Staring down with the charm Petran had given him, Marl nodded.

Dear Reader,

Thanks so much for reading the first book in the *Chronicles of the Fifth Kingdom* series. The party may have lost the battle, but the war is coming and it's far from over.

Is there another way to defeat Aldrei?

A list of strange artifacts may be the key.

But where will Marl and his friends begin?

In the Capital another battle rages. This time it's political and lines are being drawn.

If you enjoyed your trip to the *Fifth Kingdom*, you'll

adore what comes next as the world expands and alliances are forged.

Get Book Now.

www.ingramcontent.com/pod-product-compliance
Lightning Source LLC
Chambersburg PA
CBHW021215250626
47155CB00008B/2816